I0716320

A Troublesome Heart

Holly Schindler

The Original
Ruby's Place Christmas Collection

Christmas at Ruby's
I Remember You
Sentimental Journey
The Gift That Is Ruby's Place

The Spinoff Series:
Ruby's Regulars

Ruby's Story
Rare Gems
Tinsel Town
A Troublesome Heart

What You Need to Know about Ruby's Place

I get it. It's tough—often impossible—to jump into the middle of a series. Especially one that's been going on as many years as my Ruby's Place. Or, if you have been reading along, it can be hard to remember what you read three, four years ago.

Never fear. You can absolutely read *A Troublesome Heart,* even if you've never read any of the other books in the series or you feel you've lost track of the details. You only need to know (or be reminded of) a few things:

Ruby's Place is a mid-century supper club, opened in '55 by Ruby Westbrook, a ballerina who returns home following her retirement from dance. She models her establishment after some of the supper clubs she'd seen in New York. Only, in the small town of Sullivan, Missouri, everyone is a member of Ruby's club. It's a classy joint, some say once the place is open. Linen tablecloths, crystal chandeliers. The most special place in town—where people flock to celebrate holidays and special days. First dates and anniversaries. It becomes, in short, the kind of place where memories are made.

Ruby Westbrook dies in the '90s, and the building sits empty until Angela, her best friend's niece, happens by one Christmas. Angela is back in town in 2017, feeling a bit run-down. There she is, with plenty of gray in her hair and the fear that she has no great accomplishments to claim as her own. She's overcome by the memories of her youth. So much so, she decides to actually buy the empty building, and to renovate it to be an exact replica of the Ruby's Place of her memories. She even keeps the original name.

Once Angela reopens, it's clear there's something…extra-special about Ruby's Place. As some say, the "spirits" are not confined to the bottles behind the bar. On Christmas Eve, it is possible to meet up with a long-lost loved one just one more time. Say everything you didn't while they were still around—maybe *I love you* or *I'm sorry*. Others dismiss these stories, insisting it's only a mixture of the holiday and the liquor and the power of memory.

But then again, isn't memory a kind of time-traveling magic?

Most of the books in both the original four-book *Ruby's Place Christmas Collection* and the subsequent *Ruby's Regulars* series center on special Christmas Eves at Ruby's Place.

But where did this magic of memory actually come from? Turns out, any magic that exists in Ruby's Place came to life decades before Ruby bought the building—during the years when Frankie ran her speakeasy in the back.

This year's story focuses on the speakeasy days. On the foundations of the magic of Ruby's Place. And on the kindness that fed magic's roots. As kindness always has to, if magic has any kind of fighting chance.

I hope you enjoy this year's story—and I hope this Christmas, you will give someone an unexpected gift, one that means as much to them as the gifts from Hetty Bonwit meant to the town of Sullivan…

or so you're about to find out…

Happy holidays!
—*Holly*

This one is for all the tenderhearts…

Present Day

"HAVE YOU BEEN HERE before?"

It's a man who asks, and a woman who lifts her head, turning in the direction of his voice. Once, too many years gone now to be of any significance, she would have assumed he had come to flirt with her, trotting out some mangled old sweet nothing, all twisted and bent from previous use.

But she's old when he asks her, and sitting on a bench in the snow.

It seems a bit odd to him, really. Sitting there letting snow fall on her. In fact, it's what made him stop. Seeing her, he'd suspected she was not just old on the outside, but shriveled up mentally, too. Sitting here and not realizing it was barely thirty degrees out or that a good half-inch of flakes had gathered on the shoulders of her red wool coat. Maybe, he'd thought, she needed to be led back inside, where someone was looking for her and not seeing her anywhere and starting to get a little panicked.

But she smiles, and there's a sharpness in it. She knows exactly what she's doing. It is after dark on Christmas Eve. The Sullivan, Missouri square before her, lined with businesses and crowded with cars and voices and bright bulging Christmas packages tucked under arms, is a sight, one that can't be seen all in one blink. Why wouldn't she want to be out here, taking it all in? The landscape in front of her is completely decorated. Festooned, maybe. That's a better word. With vintage stars affixed to light poles and twinkling lights and gaudy silver tinsel that does not somehow look tacky but like a promise intended to be kept.

"Have you?" he repeats, honestly wanting to know now. It's no longer a way to gently find out if the woman needs some help. He senses she knows things. "Have you been here before?

She smiles. "Every Christmas Eve."

"I'm Russ," he says, extending a hand.

"You're a newspaperman," she corrects. She's a little sorry for blurting it when his face takes a tumble. He's a nice enough looking man, she realizes. Probably the girls would have warned each other about him back in her day. Whispered and called him a cad while also hoping to catch his eye. But there is something modern about his face, even though his hair is gray. Even now, she finds it startling to think that people who are themselves surely considered *old* look more modern than the faces of her youth.

"I'm not—I mean," Russ blubbers, "I *am*, I'm a reporter. But I'm not here as one tonight."

"A reporter is always a reporter. You don't turn that off," she argues.

"Are you telling me there really is a story in there?" he asks, pointing to the building behind her. "One that I'm going to want to write up?"

There is. She knows that.

"I'm at a bit of a disadvantage, ma'am. Here you know my name, but I don't know yours."

Now it's her turn to send her face tumbling. That's the last thing Hetty Bonwit—which is, in fact, her name—wants to hand over. So instead, she says, "Ruby Westbrook."

He offers her a sharp sidelong glance. "Come on, now. That's the name of the woman who used to run this place." He nods once toward the red "Ruby's Place" neon that still pulses against the pitch black night sky, right over the bright green door beside Hetty.

"What makes you so certain I'm not her?"

"Because she died some time ago. The '90s, wasn't it? That's the first thing. And I've seen pictures of her. On Christmas Eve. Pictures of her sitting on that very bench," he goes on, pointing a finger pink from the cold at the bench that Hetty is currently curled up on. "I know you're not her."

"So you have done your background," she says.

"On Christmas Eve—" Russ starts. Even with those first few introductory words, his voice takes on a rhythm that indicates he's repeating something he has heard so many times it has accidentally been committed to memory. "Yes, on Christmas Eve—Ruby Westbrook's favorite night of the year—her namesake supper club was always full of so much holiday cheer—"

"—voices all singing together," Hetty chimes in, "and children on shoulders—and homemade marshmallows—and mistletoe—and glittery gold goodness—"

"Yes!" Russ says, his face getting a little joy in it now that Hetty is playing along. "This old place of hers would be full of such holiday cheer she would have to come out here each Christmas Eve, for a moment, to catch her breath and pride herself on another successful holiday."

That, too, was all years ago. But somehow, unlike the old woman's youth, it has maintained its significance.

"Ruby's gone now," Hetty reminds him. "Has been for decades, like you said."

"Well," he admits, drawing the word out and rubbing on his chin, like maybe this is treading into dangerous territory, "that's not exactly what I hear." Russ shrugs, sheepishly, stuffing his hands in his pockets. His ears are nearly as red as the woman's coat.

"Hear?" Hetty asks, cupping her own ear. "You hear something? Carols?" She's teasing him. Music really is leaking through the glass and brick of Ruby's Place—boisterous carols being sung by everyone inside, all together. The piano rings out in-between verses.

"That's Angela who runs the place now," Russ says, looking through the plate-glass front window. "She's Ruby's niece. Don't I have that right?" He's decided to sidestep the story of Ruby. Reporter's tactic. He's trying to make her more comfortable. If she's comfortable, she'll start blabbing. Or so he hopes.

"No, Angela's the niece of Ruby's best friend," Hetty corrects. "Elizabeth Rossi, that was her aunt."

"I hear this place started as a speakeasy."

Hetty tightens up at this. It's far too close to what she personally knows about the old building—the history that, if Russ were to look close enough, he would find marked with Hetty's own fingerprints.

"Angela must know all the stories that circle around this old place," Russ adds.

That was quick, Hetty thinks. Already, here he is, coming back to the rumors. *He must really be anxious to know the truth of this place.* "Oh, Angela knows it all," Hetty agrees. "But if there's a secret to be kept, you'll never get it out of her. Not even if you could somehow cram her into one of those muddlers she uses to make drinks and threatened to smash and torture her. She would only tug on her brown knit hat, her favorite, the one her sister made, and point to one of the cardinals on the snowy windowsill. *Cardinals appear when angels are near*, she might recite, changing the subject, and offer you one of the homemade marshmallows she has perfected."

Russ likes her story. His amused expression makes the skin all along the sides of his face wrinkle. He has quite a bit of age in him. Not nearly as much as the woman, but more than she'd even suspected at first. Enough to have lost more than just a few things along the way. His heart, at this stage, is no longer raw material. It has been carved, knocked into by life's chisel.

Love has chipped some scars into him.

"It's silly, really. The holiday got to me," he says, backing up. "I shouldn't bother you. I'm sorry—you have a good Christmas, ma'am."

"You heard about Christmas Eve," Hetty calls out, before he can get away. "And how, on that one night a year, you can—well. You can speak to the dead."

"That's kind of a *not* Christmasy way of saying it," Russ tells her, returning to her, coming to stand a little closer this time.

"But that's what they say."

"Yes," he agrees, his eyes going off somewhere far away. "That's what they say."

"There's someone you would like to see," Hetty says. "Someone you have gotten all your hopes up to see. Someone you would like to see so badly, it might destroy you if you walked inside and you *didn't* see them."

He twists his face, sucks in a breath, and sighs. "Yeah," he admits, his voice lower, getting that funny sound that reveals tears are threatening to make their way in. "Yeah, there's someone I would like to see."

"You have heard that here, on Christmas Eve, there's a chance. There are stories that this is just the place for that. But then again—"

She raises her hand. She's holding a drink. Something old-fashioned looking. Sherry, maybe. Something from a Fitzgerald novel.

"—and then again," Russ says, "it might be a combination of the booze and the merriment and the magic of Christmas Eve, and maybe, in the end, all there ever was—"

"—was the *memory* of someone," they both finish at the same time.

Russ cocks his head to the side and squints at her. How could she have known he would use those exact words?

"The thing about magic," Hetty says, gripping her swizzle stick in such a way that she leaves her pinky extended, "is that it isn't a thing all on its own. It doesn't show up without asking. It doesn't *volunteer* itself."

"No?"

"It's made of ingredients," she informs him.

"That right?" he asks, drifting back to his original idea: that the woman is a bit on the daffy side. Too much time, too many years on the earth have addled her brain. Just like too many drinks.

"Well," she says, having had enough of the man and his assumptions. "You'd better go inside. If you're ever to find out the truth."

He knows he's offended her, and he wants to make up. But he supposes there never was such a thing—with a stranger there was only politeness, but when you breeched that, it was over. And so the only thing left to do is to go inside, as she said.

"Merry Christmas," she offers as his hand touches the door.

And he stops—because he could have sworn that her voice

sounded funny, tinny. Almost like a music box.

But he shrugs it off—probably, her voice hit the edge of her cocktail glass. Kind of like how a wet fingertip could make that funny ringing sound when it circled the rim.

Hetty smiles to herself. It's enough if she's the only person who knows the truth.

Russ disappears inside.

Hetty closes her eyes and takes a long sip. The door to Ruby's Place swings open and shut beside her a few times.

Magic—at least, the magic of Ruby's Place—*did* come together through a mixture of ingredients. Just like her own cocktail, that bitter and sweet tang that touches her tongue as she raises her glass on that cold Christmas Eve night.

She knows all about the magic of Ruby's Place.

"Are you an ingredient?"

Hetty's eyes pop open again. And there he is—Russ—back staring down at her.

Hetty grins. She is. But before she can consider whether or not she actually wants to answer, her mind drifts back to the little boy who was also an ingredient—every bit as strong and necessary as she was. And she knows that together, their story is maybe the most important part of how this Christmas Eve's Ruby's Place came to be.

1.

November 23, 1938

WALTER HADN'T EXPECTED THE first tinge of holiday red to be found on a dead body. But there it was, just the same, the poor blackbird slaughtered surely by the Bonwit cat, lying with its beak in the mud, its lifeless eye offering him a sad blank stare.

He could feel cracks forming across his heart as he stared back. Poor thing. Just trying to go about his day. And he got killed for it. Walter raised a foot—throbbing and aching and stinging against the cold—and toed some snow over the blackbird's body.

And then it was back to the chore at hand, which was simply

getting home. Easy enough. Or it should have been.

But Walter hesitated at the edge of the muddy path stuck between two silvery bumpers of snow. The entire length couldn't have been more than—what? Half the distance between first and second base out at the baseball diamond he and the rest of the kids had laid out in the empty lot behind their neighborhood? Still, he couldn't do it. He could not walk down that path. Not now that he had made the mistake of looking up at the old Victorian house right there beside him. Hetty Bonwit's towering three-story with the gingerbread trim along the edge of the roof. That's what his dad had called it, anyway. Gingerbread. But the trim was beginning to look more and more like eyebrows to Walter, the kind that were all wrinkled up in anger and annoyance. The kind that could only be found above eyes that dared, *Go on and do it. You'll be sorry.*

"Don't be so dopey about it," his best friend Petey groaned, flicking his cigarette ash into a half-melted footprint, one of a hundred that had already been tamped into the path by the rest of the neighborhood. "This stretch here doesn't even belong to that old Bonwit lady."

"Hetty," Walter said.

"Fine. Hetty. She likes to have an excuse to act like some mean old junkyard dog, ever since her husband died. She has no right to yell at us about coming this way. No bite. Right? Everybody knows that."

That much was true, but it didn't make what Walter had to do any easier. He wished he could be more like Petey, who at ten was already an expert on swearing and spitting and never seemed to flinch at anything harsh or mean. Maybe, Walter had often thought, it was because Petey lived above a funeral home, with all those dead bodies coming in and out, all of them possessing, at that point, only the secrets they would take with them to the grave. Maybe it had all been cold enough to harden Petey, like some sort of perpetual winter floating up from the basement, freezing his heart in his sleep.

"Here," Petey said, sticking his cigarette into the side of his mouth and squinting against the smoke curling into his eyes. "Don't forget this." He reached into his coat pocket and tugged out a magazine page, folded into fourths. The ad Petey had torn from his own dime-store copy of *Open Roads for Boys* magazine, the one for Ball-Band sport shoes. The ad promised Ball-Band canvas shoes got lots of mileage and had a STA-KLEEN insole. Walter's mother, Petey had promised, would be won over by that.

Looking at the page in Petey's hand made Walter's feet throb all over again. He needed new shoes. He needed a lot, actually—his coat puckered when he tried to button it and his pants were an inch too short. But it was the shoes that were killing him. At this point, he'd actually lost track of how long he'd needed new shoes. Three weeks ago, he'd traded his school shoes for his lace-up official Boy Scout shoes, because for some reason, they seemed to have been sized slightly bigger. It had been okay for a little while. But Walter was growing so fast that his feet were now big enough to have actually stretched the leather a good half inch or so beyond the edge of the soles. They cut into his heels and pinched against his toes, and in the cold, the ache was nearly unbearable.

"Thanks," Walter said, sliding the ad from Petey's fingers. This thing with the ad showed living in a funeral home hadn't made Petey entirely hard inside just yet.

"Shoulda hit your mom up for new shoes when I told you the first time," Petey scolded around his cigarette. Trying, Walter figured, not to look too mushy, helping Walter out with his shoes and all.

Petey was lucky because he was small. Everything in the world was big on him. He never grew out of anything. Heck, he wore handed-down clothes out before he even had time to grow into them. His mother replaced dungarees with ripped knees as soon as she found them in the laundry. He didn't know what it was like to have to tell parents you needed new anything.

"You waited too long to fess up," Petey pressed.

But it was a terrible time to need such things, Walter knew. "Tomorrow's Thanksgiving," he tried to justify. "Mom saved up for dinner."

"Right," Petey said. "And then after that, she'll be trying to scrape up for Christmas. There's not gonna be a time when she magically has any more money."

The afternoon sun pelted them through their woolen hats, knitted by grandmothers.

"So are you coming?" Petey pressed, taking a step toward the muddy path. The shortcut to their street.

"I still think we could go on the other side."

"Of what? Her house? Have you looked over there recently?" Petey asked. "The dump where everybody in the neighborhood brings their junk. You want to go there."

Only, it wasn't really junk. It was sort of half-junk. Busted furniture and wooden crates, glass bottles and tin cans, broken-up radios, bundled-up newspapers. All things that could be given a second life. Even the newspapers could be used for insulation or to start fires in the fireplace.

"She lets people come by on that side."

"But then what? We're supposed to jump off the ten-foot retaining wall to get to the street?"

"I have time to go around the block," Walter said, looking up once more at the frowning gingerbread.

"Yeah, but can you stand it?" Petey pointed down toward Walter's feet.

He couldn't. The cold was a metal vice against his toes. He'd hoped they would go numb. But he hadn't been so lucky.

"Don't be such a tenderheart," Petey said.

"That's what Mom calls me."

"I know," Petey said. "I thought it would make you mad enough to finally get a move on."

Walter let out a breathy laugh and shook his head. The two of them knew that the tender heart of Walter's was how they'd become such good friends. Petey lived in the creepy house, as boys on weekend baseball diamonds used to say right to Petey's face. That was the one thing that really seemed to get to him. Pinch his skin, make his eyes water. Walter hadn't been able to stand the look of hurt on his face. Walter being kind when no one else was—that had won him his very best bud.

"Come on," Petey prodded. "Maybe, if we make her come running out, she'll fall in that big old hole in her front step. That'd be a sight."

"Yeah," Walter murmured.

"So are you gonna go or what?" Petey asked, losing patience.

"I will," Walter said, his voice embarrassingly high-pitched.

"*Jiminy Cricket*," Petey swore, tossing his cigarette to the snow. "I'm going." And he began to tromp down the path, his feet squishing in sun-melted shallow puddles.

Walter was attacked by the familiar burst of fear that always hit him when he felt Petey might be drifting away. And so he hugged his school books tighter and he trudged forward. But now that he was moving again, he found that his shoes had grown metal teeth, the kind that were in traps out in the woods, and with each step, the jaw snapped shut on him all over again.

It was such a tiny little stretch he needed to walk. His house was getting so close now. But his shoes weren't just tight. Or thin. Or ill-fitting. They were cutting. Digging. Snapping with metal teeth. Blood leeched up from the heels of his socks.

It was the only reason why he'd taken this shortcut before. The one next to old Hetty Bonwit's house. Petey was right. With shoes that tight, Walter couldn't take the long way around. Not anymore. Even though Hetty Bonwit had been coming after all the children—well, everyone, really, who tried to take this shortcut along the edge of her house—but the children especially, it seemed to Walter. As soon as she spied anyone there through the slit in one of her curtains, the front door would bang open and she would burst onto the porch, cradling her cat to her chest, her shrill scream tearing at the air. Waving her arms. Shooing them away. Shaking her fists. Occasionally banging a cooking pot against her porch railing. Calling them all trespassers.

But the thing was, the last time he'd taken the shortcut, Hetty had burst from her house in tears. "Why can't you go away?" she'd pleaded. "This is my house. Mine."

Those tears had cut into Walter. He'd had no idea this was upsetting her so much. Not like this. For the most part, he'd thought she was only griping. Barking for attention, like Petey said.

But she was hurt, he'd realized, with a pang that reverberated all the way through him. It had *hurt* her that they were taking this shorter route down the side of her property. "I'm sorry," Walter had told her. And he'd meant it. "I'll go the other way from now on. I promise."

And now, here he was, his best friend goading him into this shortcut again. Not even two days after making that very promise.

He took a step, but the teeth of his shoes sliced through him, so deep he felt it all the way down to the bone. He was bleeding. A man who'd stepped on a wolf trap couldn't be expected to walk to work before taking off his shoes, could he?

Walter leaned down, attacking the laces.

His feet stung. And burned. And had been stuck in a vice. Tighter and tighter and bones and skin were breaking and bleeding and his skin was surely going blue.

"What are you doing?" Petey called. "Walt!"

But he needed to get them off. Anything was better than this. Walking home in his socks. It would be better. He had to get them off. *Please God,* Walter said silently, *if you let me get out of these shoes, I'll do anything. I'll turn back and go the long way around again. I won't take the shortcut. I'll keep my word to Hetty. Okay?*

As he worked the laces, he could hear the front door bang open at the old Victorian. He could hear her voice, that high pitched wail: *"You!"*

Still bent over, Walter twisted his neck to glance in the direction of the voice. There she was, Hetty Bonwit, all seven hundred years of her, ambling toward him, her face a vicious snarl.

Today, she came armed with a broom. "This is my house," she cried out. "My house!" And she began to swing that broom at Walter like a regular Lou Gehrig.

There was such hate in her. It was the hatred that hurt, far more than the ill-fitting shoes and the wet cold. He hadn't even wanted to come this way. Didn't she know that? Didn't she know that Petey had been the one to insist? Couldn't she see him out there, trying to untie his shoes? Couldn't she tell that he was in pain—every bit as much as she was? Didn't she have any compassion for *him?*

What if he couldn't get another pair of shoes? What if there was no money for that? What if he would have to wear these shoes another week or so, to give his parents time to save? He was in pain.

His feet were in snares. And he'd wanted to keep his promise, but he couldn't. Hadn't she seen him limp?

He put all those questions into his eyes as he stared at her through the arms he'd thrown up to protect his head from the swinging broom.

"You selfish boy. *Selfish*," she told him. She took another step closer and snarled, "*Get out.*"

Her words sliced straight into his soft spots. And Walter knew for certain how that poor blackbird wound up in the current shape he was in.

A SHRIEK MADE BERNARD jerk, his head banging against one of the hinged panels of the Model T hood.

Another shriek and he was already on his way, rubbing the sore spot on the top of his head, racing past the dusty fenders and out of the garage behind the Bonwit home.

It was the rage in Hetty's voice that brought the panic, fiery across his chest. He had to help her. His sweet Hetty. The sound of her pain—wasn't anger a kind of pain, really?—always hurt him.

The December chill attacked him; his pulsing skull sent his thoughts in a confused tumble. In the distance, he could hear a train whistle.

It was the whistle that made him slow down, reconsider what was happening. Was the whistle all he had ever heard? It had never been Hetty screaming at all?

He had only started to relax when he rounded the far edge of the large Bonwit porch, and saw two young boys. Bernard tossed his socket wrench—the same he had been using to inspect the Model T's spark plugs—into the snow. He didn't want the boys telling some story that he had gone after them, threatening them with a weapon.

He had to get Hetty out of there, away from the interlopers—Hetty's favorite word for anyone who used the stretch beside her house as a shortcut.

Hetty shook her angry fist. Those boys had probably said something awful to her. Children always did—like she was nothing more than some inanimate object, a scarecrow that couldn't care less if you punched its stomach, because it had been made of nothing but hay.

Hetty would care, though. She would care because their words *would* hurt.

One of the boys—the one Bernard had scolded the other day for knocking cigarette ash onto the newspapers on the other side of their house—began to open his mouth.

Bernard sprinted closer. He needed to get her back inside.

That was how kindness worked, after all. Or so he had learned many times the past four decades. Kindness was—well, it was sort of springy. It didn't just land—it bounced and it carried you forward, and suddenly, there you were, trying to return grace of some sort to the person who had been good to you.

The boys standing there at the side of the house would never have believed it, but there had been plenty of kindnesses that Hetty had extended toward Bernard—forty years' worth. That was why he was so protective of her—he was not merely a housekeeper, but a friend. A family member, almost. One who loved Hetty, who wanted to shield her from the winter of people's cruelty.

The truth was, the people of Sullivan should have all wanted to feel this way toward Hetty. So many of them had been helped by the Bonwits. But the hard times had turned their memories hazy. Looking backward these days, they saw nothing but sick cloudy glass.

Bernard remembered, though. He remembered with the clarity of a recorded document, each of the Bonwit generosities written in an imaginary ledger in his mind.

Behind Bernard, a distant train whistle blew again. And it was back with him—that first day on the train, the day he had arrived in Sullivan. The feeling of pure excitement burning in him like a swallow of Old Tom gin.

A man had taken up the seat beside him. A small man, the kind who gave off the air of a folded handkerchief in a pocket—compact, always there if you needed it. Bernard had actually chuckled at himself for even thinking it. Laughter came easily to him that day, because at eighteen, he had suddenly found himself a man ready to start his adult life. On his own, for the first time.

"On your way to Sullivan?" he'd asked the man at his side.

"I am at that. Gent Bonwit," he'd answered, extending his hand. He had a musical voice, and wore a suit of impeccable tailoring. Bernard noticed immediately when he shook his hand. The jacket sleeve had fine, even stitching that ended right at the wrist bone, allowing for a quarter inch of cuff to show through. A precise fit.

Bernard's eyes were attuned to such things, as his grandfather had been a tailor.

"You live there? In Sullivan, that is?" Bernard had asked, brightening.

"I do. With my wife, Hetty."

"Perhaps you know my cousin? He's what's bringing me to Sullivan."

"Coming for the holiday?" Gent asked.

This was always Bernard's favorite part of the memory—the

fact that it was Christmas. It gave the whole scene a sweet, almost fated feel to it, looking back. The windows were steamed and the train car actually smelled like pine. One of the passengers had attached a little bell to their luggage handle, and it jingled in rhythm as the wheels spun across the rails.

"No. I'm coming to Sullivan to live," Bernard announced, a silly proud smile on his face. Then, as he leaned in closer, "He is quite the big deal in Sullivan. My cousin, that is."

"Is that right?"

Bernard did not know it at the time, but the expression on Gent's face was one of amusement rather than awe or admiration. It did not take many days in Sullivan before a man realized there really was no such thing as a big deal inside the city limits. That was how Gent always put it, anyway. *None of us are big deals.* How many times Bernard would hear that over the next few decades. Others in Sulli-van—say, the women in the local milliner's shop, gossiping away as they tried on the latest hat—preferred to think they were all big deals.

Funny, Bernard would later realize, how two things were really one and the same. After all, if *everyone* was important, then *no one* was.

"His name is Henry Whitaker," Bernard said.

Gent simply stared at him, his amused expression ever so slowly evaporating. Henry Whitaker was the town drunk, often found in the early morning hours in the police station.

"He is being asked to run for office," Bernard disclosed. "I'm coming to work for him now. He's got a job for me."

"He told you he did?" Gent asked.

"Oh, he writes to my family often. He has said many times that when I'm grown, I should come straight to Sullivan. He would take care of me."

"Letters to the family," Gent mused. And Bernard didn't

know it, not then anyway, but Gent was thinking about how badly Henry must have needed to be a real somebody—a somebody above all others. Such status, of course, was an impossibility for anyone in Sullivan, but especially for Henry Whitaker. Poor Henry, making a life for himself in family epistles, a life in which he was no longer a man in a drunk tank or a man being dragged off a park bench where he'd fallen asleep or a man passed out on the corner outside of the Sullivan saloon or the man being pointed to by the city's temperance activists as example number one why whiskey was evil.

Gent listened as Bernard told him all about his hopes and how he had come from a farm and how his whole life had been walking behind a plow and feeling the scorch of the sun and the burn of the winter. And how he had always dreamed of a city, and even if Sullivan wasn't Kansas City, there was still electricity on the square and a fancy theater with Sunday matinées and luscious food and afternoons to look forward to at the mayor's family home.

He could not wait to be part of such a society, Bernard had said, young fool that he was. And he could not wait to see the look on his cousin's face when he showed up unannounced, taking him up on the offer he had been making for years.

Gent had listened to it all.

And when the train came to a stop, Gent had simply said, "My wife Hetty and I have a carriage house out back. It's always open to guests such as yourself. People new to town." He said this even though it was not entirely true. Even though the carriage house was where people stayed when they found themselves in bad times. Dire straits—that was the term often used. When they had no options, and they had no money, and there was time, but what did time matter if you had no direction?

Direction was to be found in that carriage house. Or so its

former inhabitants all said.

Bernard hesitated—why would he take up with strangers when his cousin was right there in town?

"You don't want to impose on him so late in the day," Gent explained. "Why, the time to show up is tomorrow morning. And you know," Gent added, "come to think of it, I do believe our carriage house would really be the proper place for you to stay until you get on your feet. Why, you would prefer not to have to ride on a single person's coattails, depend on them literally for everything. Isn't that right? Everyone needs that hand to get started, but this would also prove to your cousin that you were quite resourceful all on your own. Quite deserving of his good graces."

Bernard nodded, reluctantly. He was feeling more like his gangly eighteen-year-old self. Living on his own—as he had never done before—was a little frightening, now that the reality of it was tapping him on the shoulder. Cousin Henry was as much a stranger to him as anyone milling about at the depot. He feared his farm-boy ways might look backward to his upper-crust cousin. It would be nice to get the feel of a real city while living with someone he did not feel the need to impress. But did he trust this man?

"Mr. Bonwit," the conductor greeted as the two men stepped onto the platform. "Fine evening to return to Sullivan, isn't it?"

"It is," Gent agreed. He took a deep breath and glanced about the depot. "Something about a fresh snow makes the world look new again."

"Tell Mrs. Bonwit hello," the conductor said.

But before the conductor could get away, Gent announced, pushing the boy forward, "I would like to introduce Bernard Whitaker. Our guest. In the *carriage house*."

The conductor raised his eyebrows in a silent agreement not

to press the issue. Everyone in Sullivan knew the true purpose of the Bonwits' carriage house.

"Mr. Whitaker, what a lucky man you are, indeed," the conductor said. "Not a finer place to stay in all of Sullivan than the Bonwit carriage house. And no better company."

Company? Come to think of it, that would be nice, too—not to have to be all alone. And the conductor knew Gent? If the conductor knew him, did everyone in town know Gent?

"Just until he gets on his feet," Gent told the conductor.

"Just until," Bernard had agreed, finally, in that moment, making his first true decision. Not quite a man completely on his own—and with that came not disappointment but a surge of relief.

Now, forty years later, he was still in the Bonwit home—no longer living in the carriage house, but a resident of the actual house. On the ground floor, in the room beside the stairs, two floors below the Bonwits' room. That cousin of his had died of dropsy thirty-five years ago. There had never been a job.

But Gent had known that would be the case.

Bernard cleared his throat as he rounded the edge of the Bonwit home, making his presence known to the two boys taunting Hetty. When the boys turned their attention toward him, they began to back up. The boy with the cigarettes narrowed his eyes, but his friend grabbed his arm and dragged him, limping all the way.

"Ma'am," Bernard said, his hand on Hetty's elbow. "Might I help you up the porch steps?"

She sighed, and even though her face was filled with little hairline wrinkles, he could still see her as she had looked that first day, when Gent had brought him home. How she had smelled of lilacs and she had hummed throwing open the door of the carriage house. She'd had red hair and the clearest green eyes he'd ever seen. Everything about her had been so fluid, so easy—as she'd moved, her steps had seemed more of a waltz than a walk.

That afternoon, though, as Bernard attempted to help Hetty, he could not quite recall when the easiness had left her. He only knew it had been a long time since the woman had moved without effort. She was covered in rusty hinges, any attempted movement made still harder by the harsh December weather.

He led her inside, where he felt the weight of her sadness. It always crashed into her when she stepped inside her house and had to take in the sparse interior.

Gent's passing only a handful of years ago had left Hetty with debts that required the selling-off of anything even remotely valuable. At that point, she was down to only her most worthless belongings: a grandfather clock that did not keep the right time anymore. The Victorian settee, threadbare and, after having been used as a scratching post by every stray cat the Bonwits had welcomed, sprouting horsehair stuffing and a couple of springs.

And the occasionally-running Model T, of course. Out in the garage.

A few visitors would make the home feel full again. It hurt Bernard the way everyone kept their distance now.

"I've been working on the car, ma'am. Trying to get to the bottom of why it sputters and coughs."

"If you can fix it, maybe we could still sell it," she murmured, yet again. "Too bad we didn't get it sold before Thanksgiving. You deserve a fine Thanksgiving, Bernard."

Bernard's heart broke. "You deserve a fine Thanksgiving, too, ma'am."

Hetty's eyes darted up at him, slightly surprised—but only slightly. That tone of his made it clear what he really meant. Hetty deserved a fine Thanksgiving, especially here, with time winding down for her.

They both knew it.

The Hetty that Bernard had met all those years ago had behaved as though she'd had all the time in the world—but wasn't that the illusion of life? It was always finite, but when the woman was young, and her entire lifespan could still easily triple and maybe even then some, time felt as big as the sky. The end a tiny spec on the horizon, one that could never catch up to her.

Yes, it was life's great optical illusion. The end was always closer than anyone ever imagined.

Now, here, a rusty gate, Hetty knew this better than most anyone in Sullivan. She was uncomfortably close to that jumping-off point, and she saw life for everything it was. Mostly, she thought of it as a cruel joke. Like everyone else, this body of hers was never built to let her do everything she would like. A young body still had to pause to sleep and eat. Young minds still needed a cooling-off period, so many empty hours of goofing off and playing around. It only cut into what little time you were granted at the beginning.

There was always so, so little time.

And what did a woman do, with what little time she had?

"I want to spend whatever I have left in peace," she told Bernard as her cat, Reginald, began to circle about her legs. "Those boys—I didn't know who they were when I went outside. I was afraid it was someone else. Yet another unpaid bill, yet another debt of Gent's. I have done everything I can to settle up. What if someone shows up wanting to take this house? What will happen to us then?"

Perhaps Hetty remembered somewhere deep down that such a visit was on its way. Perhaps she had been dreading it—perhaps the details were slightly fuzzy. Perhaps some of her memory was getting cloudy glass, too. Maybe she had attempted to place any of life's unpleasantness behind that cloudy spot. Maybe she had aimed to forget.

But it all came back to her—back into focus—when the front
door rattled beneath a fierce knock.

"Mrs. Bonwit?" a voice called from the porch. "It's Mr. Pulcheck, ma'am. Your husband's attorney."

"MRS. BONWIT?" THE MAN outside continued to shout. "Mrs. Bonwit!"

"I can't do this, Bernard," Hetty said. "I can't go through another fight. There's no money left to fight over. This has been going on for *years*. How many more debts could he have had?"

Bernard edged closer to the door.

"Mrs. Bonwit? Please open up. I must tell you something. Please."

Bernard reached closer to the doorknob, raising his eyebrows.

Hetty shook her head.

"Mrs. Bonwit, Mrs. Bonwit. I have a story to tell you."

Hetty only clenched her fists.

In the center of the door, the metal flap of the letter drop swung open. "Fine," Mr. Pulcheck said, a sliver of his face visible through the open slot. "Don't open up. But you will listen to me, here. You will let me tell you this. Your husband came to me, Mrs. Bonwit.

Before his untimely demise."

"He was seventy-two," Hetty scoffed. "Hardly untimely."

"I don't care about *years*, Mrs. Bonwit. A man such as Gent—why, when he goes, it is always untimely."

Hetty softened, agreeing.

"I must tell you that he left you something, Mrs. Bonwit. Something beyond unpaid debt. I have spent the last few years in search of it. And I have not been able to uncover it. But Mrs. Bonwit—"

"You don't know what you're talking about," Hetty interrupted. "He had nothing."

"That's not true!" Mr. Pulcheck shouted through the mail drop. "Mrs. Bonwit, please let me inside. We need to discuss this."

"What a fool you are," Hetty said. "He had nothing, do you hear me? Nothing." She moved in a jerky, painful way toward the door, where she pushed the metal flap of the mail drop back down.

"Mrs. Bonwit!" came the muffled shout. "You're making a mistake."

"Tomorrow is Thanksgiving, Mr. Pulcheck," Hetty said. "Time to go home to your family."

She remained at the door, tense and angry.

"I'll be back, Mrs. Bonwit," he promised.

"Watch out for the rotten front step," she shouted, and stayed at the door until his footsteps faded and he had safely gone.

"Can you believe him?" she asked. "What fiction!"

She began to laugh then—the first time in months that Bernard had heard any such sound from her. When she finally wound down, she said, "How about a little tea, Bernard? I—"

She stopped, mid-sentence, startled. Bernard knew exactly what had rattled her—his ghostly white face.

"What's the matter, Bernard?"

"Gent did leave you something, Mrs. Bonwit. But I'm afraid—
I'm afraid I'm the one that may have wrecked everything."

28

4.

"WHAT DO YOU MEAN, he left me something?" Hetty whispered.

Bernard fought the urge to wring his hands. Or rub his face. He fought tears, too. And the ache of this thing he had carried with him even before Gent had died.

"Gent's store was doing poorly," Bernard started.

"Gent's store always did poorly," Hetty corrected. Was she standing straighter? It seemed to Bernard that she was. She had found strength in this—or was it anger, maybe?—already, before she knew the full story.

"This was right before he had to close." They both felt it, at the same time: the sinking in the chest that had accompanied the loss of Gent's music box store. There really was a specific kind of weight that only showed up when something you loved went missing. Strange, how the heaviest things in the world were the things that were no longer around.

"It was a lovely life, there in the store with him. All those years I worked there," Bernard insisted.

"It was a lovely life here," Hetty said.

"Gent and his music boxes," Bernard said.

And Hetty smiled that far-away smile that said she was drifting off, back to something long gone by then. Drifting toward the echo of the old sensation that had always bloomed in her chest upon seeing Gent—that warm swell of comfort and thrill. "They always fascinated me," she said. "How a little spinning metal wheel covered in bumps could pluck the proper notes of any melody. Beethoven or popular songs or carols."

"But no one ever came to the store—not hardly, anyway."

"My father didn't want me to marry him. Not a silly little music box maker," she admitted.

"He had built so much, your father. He wanted you to have every bit as much. That's all."

"Yes," Hetty said, pleased Bernard remembered the stories she had told him over the years. "He had built a lot."

"People always say money doesn't grow on trees, but for your father, it did," Bernard went on, carrying Hetty into the warm pool of pleasant memories.

She smiled. "It really did. All that lumber after the Civil War, all those bridges that had to be rebuilt throughout the state."

"And then the wise investment in the railroad."

"Money seemed a game to me when I was little," Hetty admitted. "The way one marble could win you fifty from the other children in the park if you played it right."

Bernard laughed. He hadn't heard that tidbit before. Maybe it had just come to Hetty.

"We had so many parties right here," Hetty said, pointing at

the threadbare remnants of her life. And as she said it, it was all coming back—the plush sleeves of her favorite burgundy velvet dress.
The music and clink of crystal glasses and cheers that followed toasts.
She had been a shy girl, the kind to want to drift to the fringes of parties. But in her own home, during those days, the right gathering could
transform her. Make her feel unusually beautiful.

"And a wedding, too," Bernard reminded her. Not that she
needed reminding.

"Yes, the winter wedding. All those amaryllis all over the foy-
er. Despite Father's hesitance. 'Why this one, after all this time?' he'd
asked. But there had only ever been one. There only needed to be
one."

"He knew how much you loved him."

"And he had always been such a gentleman. It was why the
nickname, ever since he was a boy. *Gent.*"

"And so he came to live with you and your parents, right here."

"The four of us in this big old sprawling place."

"And he opened his store."

"The store."

They both went round and round, spinning, their memories
like the metal wheel of one of Gent's music boxes—playing the melody of Gent's life.

Maybe, Bernard thought, if Gent were in the room with them,
there would be a softness in the hard, heartbreaking story he needed
to tell.

"How I loved working with Gent in the music box store,"
Bernard said. "I was only supposed to be the occasional counter man,
but my shirtsleeves were rolled and sawdust was in my pockets at the
end of my days there, too. Gent taught me how to do a bit of carving.
How to make each box special. Match a piece to a customer's wish.

And he taught me a bit about how to fix the boxes that came back broken. That happened more than people came in to buy new ones. Boxes got knocked off of dressers or clumsy children played too hard with the delicate pieces."

"Never for a fee, though," Hetty murmured. "Never. Not with Gent. If Gent made the box originally, the repair was completed at no cost, regardless of age. Replaced if the box was beyond repair."

"The store was mostly empty," Bernard told her. "But it never felt that way. Not with Gent there."

"No one was ever lonely with Gent around," she agreed.

"When your parents died, he insisted no one ever be allowed to be lonely. Including me."

"Yes," she whispered. "The years of my youth, they glittered. So many parties. So many important people. And then, with Gent—a mere music-box maker—it could have all ended. Should have ended. But people still came. A different sort of person."

"People like me," Bernard said. "People who had slipped up, made mistakes. Simply coming to Sullivan—that could have been an enormous mistake for me. But because of Gent, it wasn't."

"They knocked on our door when their pockets were empty of everything, including hope." Sullivan had forgotten this—oh, of all the horrible things to happen to Hetty, they had *forgotten* this. They had let this new Hetty—the one terrified of losing her home to yet another of Gent's unpaid debts, some hidden loan bubbling up to the surface—replace everything they had known of her before. It turned out to be so easy to sour a memory—to curdle it, like vinegar in milk.

They had forgotten, but Hetty hadn't.

Neither had Bernard. How could he?

"Trouble is always around," Bernard said, continuing on with the story of the carriage house. "Trouble could be found long before these last few lean years. Trouble can always wreak its havoc on one poor soul or another. But the Bonwit door was never bolted, not against anyone who had ever stumbled."

"Gent had insisted on it," Hetty agreed. "'Let them stay,' he was always saying. 'We're lucky. They can have some of our luck. We have no children to give it to and the two of us could never use it all.'"

Ever so slowly, their smiles faded.

"But he did, in fact, use it all," Bernard said.

"My father would have so much to say to me now," Hetty lamented. "His fears were well-founded."

"He helped us all a little too much. Once your father's money was gone, he borrowed to continue helping."

When Gent had died, there had been nothing left. He'd lost more than money—he lost face, even from the grave. He lost a kind of small-town fame he had acquired for helping. Stories had float-ed through town—gossip had horrible wings, like a flock of black-birds—that Gent had committed suicide. Other men had met such fate during those times. But Gent had not. He would never. He had tried to hang on. But there was nothing, in the end, to clutch onto.

"And now, just as my father feared. Penniless," Hetty said.

She wandered over to a curio cabinet—one of many that had been built to house Gent's music boxes. "It was one of the greatest sadnesses of my life to have to sell so many of them. I only wish I knew what happened to that first box he ever made. It was always my favorite. It played—"

"'Let Me Call You Sweetheart,'" Bernard finished.

"How did you know?" Hetty whispered, her eyes as large as a child's. "It was broken before you even came to stay."

"I was in charge of the tickets—which kept track of rightful ownership for the boxes needing repair."

"I know all this," Hetty told him. "I know how the store worked. You think I could have ever forgotten?"

"It had been getting close to evening, on a Christmas Eve, and there we were, our shirt sleeves rolled and our brooms whisking over the floor. Even on Christmas, Gent loved his work so much. And before we started to lock up, I asked Gent, I said, 'Shouldn't we put a ticket on this one?' One of the broken boxes. And he said no—it wasn't a customer's. It was yours. He told me all about it. I remember, I said how pleased you would be to learn that he was finally fixing it. But he had taken everything out inside. Even the mechanism."

Bernard make a motion with his hands, as though he were holding that music box and pointing out the missing wheel. "I asked him what use it was if it couldn't play music anymore. He said there was magic in good things. In revisiting them in your mind. I didn't know what he meant, but Gent was always either whistling or talking in riddles and I—"

"Ber*nard*." Hetty didn't have patience for details. Not now.

"He asked me to take it to the bank. Said he couldn't wait one more moment to get home to you. Said the day had gotten away from him before he could take it himself. That he had been meaning to take it for quite some time already. Weeks, I think he said. But it was always one thing or another—besides, *you* know Gent and the bank. Gent and money."

"*Yes*. Gent and money."

"A broken music box! It didn't make sense. But Gent said, 'If things ever get bad for my Hetty and I'm not around, you can tell her to go get it from our safe deposit box.'"

"And did you?" Hetty asked, a tear already trailing down her face.

"I—Mrs. Bonwit, I meant to. I trusted Gent. I thought surely—even if his intention wasn't quite clear at the moment, eventually, it would be. But you have to know—it was Christmas. And I saw Ida. You know Ida—she's the cook at the Pendleton place. You know I've done landscaping at the Pendletons' every spring and summer since I arrived in Sullivan."

"Yes?"

"I intended to go to the bank. I did. But I was already pressed for time. And Ida—we'd worked together so long. As much as I loved working for Gent, it was always so important to me to contribute to the household here, in my own way, and the Pendletons…"

Hetty drew in a sharp breath.

"Well. I've always loved Ida. And Ida was going to be alone that night. I couldn't have that. Not the whole night. So I went with her—to Frankie's."

"The speakeasy."

"Right. When I got there, Frankie asked me if I wanted to put that old music box behind the bar. And I did. Safekeeping, you know. And, oh, Mrs. Bonwit, you should have seen it that night. How everyone celebrated. And loved on Ida. She was the one, you know, who could mix drinks so that they were palatable. Because Frankie only had—"

"Bathtub gin," Hetty whispered.

"Yes."

"And it got late," she supposed.

"Yes."

"Too late for you to go to the bank."

"Yes."

"So you did what?"

"I left it. There. I didn't mean to. I got about halfway home when I realized it. And then I thought I would turn around—but like you said, it was too late for the bank, anyway. So I thought I'd go the day after Christmas. Frankie would keep it safe. Besides, who would want to steal it? It was a broken music box."

"What Christmas Eve was this?" Hetty asked, her eyes closed.

"1931."

"The same Christmas Eve of the speakeasy raid."

And there it was, suddenly—the story of that awful Christmas Eve shootout. Blood on the floor of the speakeasy. A tragedy that had rocked the soul of Sullivan. Bernard's mouth was nearly too dry to utter the single syllable: "Yes."

"The Christmas Eve when Frankie's was shut down for good."

"Yes."

"And you never went back? Never?"

"Mrs. Bonwit, please. You must know that I would have, but—it was a broken music box."

"You don't think that Gent might have had a reason?" she hissed, furious. "You don't think there was something—?"

"I couldn't tell him. I couldn't admit to it. And then—after so much time—surely it wouldn't be there anymore. In the shuffle of the city taking over the building and trying to rent it out. A broken box!"

"There's no way Gent would leave me without it. Not like this. He would be *sure* I would get it back. If it's important, it has to be within reach."

"Mrs. Bonwit, I'm telling you—it's not."

"This can't be right. None of it's right. Gent wouldn't leave me this way."

"Mrs. Bonwit, please."

"I'll *find* it. Give me the key," Hetty demanded. "Give me the key to the storage room."

"HETTY," BERNARD PLEADED—A rare use of her first name. "Please don't do this." Her desperation was stretching at his heart, tugging to the point that tiny little tears were showing up. His heart would rip in half if she continued.

"It can't be lost," she insisted. "It can't be."

"It is. I lost it," Bernard whispered, his lips turning red and a grimace forming.

"Gent would not allow that."

"He wouldn't. But I did. I failed him. And you."

"Give me the *keys*, Bernard."

She held out her gnarled hand.

Bernard reached into his pocket and retrieved it from the circle of keys he carried always.

She snatched it up—an old-fashioned brass key with ornate looping circles on the end—and limped toward the storage room, the rusty hinges of her knees and hips fighting her as she ambled down the long corridor.

Even the rustiest gate could find the ability to move if a force pushed on it hard enough. Hetty's determination was a force greater than any Missouri storm wind.

Behind the door, a sea of shelves and boxes. The musty smell of time having been locked away.

"It's all here," Bernard marveled. "Every last thing?"

"Of course it all is," Hetty said, her knobby fingers reaching to the first shelf.

"Surely, this must be worth quite a bit. All of this in here," Bernard said. Because he knew these were the trinkets the Bonwit guests had exchanged for time in the carriage house out back. Bernard had paid for his keep in work. Others had bartered with items.

"Of course it isn't. None of these things are worth a dime," Hetty snapped at him.

"It's a mistake," she muttered to herself. "The music box has to be here somewhere. Gent would have made sure of that before he went."

"But these things were for room and board—"

"Do you honestly think Gent would take something that could have been sold? These people who came here, looking for help, they had nothing. But Gent let them keep their pride and pay for their stay or loan in trinkets. Not a loan, though, that's not right. Never a loan. Aid, maybe," she corrected herself. "But he let them give him worthless things. *Anything.* That way, it wasn't a handout. He took whatever they had as payment. Costume jewelry or clogged-up foun-tain pens. Watches that would no longer wind. Picture frames missing pictures—and glass."

"So it—it's all worthless?" Bernard asked, his hope losing col-or again. For a moment, he had sworn he'd seen an end to their poverty. The Pendleton job wouldn't kick in again until the spring, and he had begun to worry the two of them would have to scrounge for food through the winter like stray cats.

"They were meaningful only to the person who had given it away," Hetty said. "Gent had judged the value based on how hard it would be to part with it. " She panted, staring out at the sea of things, tears forming yet again.

She would have crumpled into a heap on the floor, but she knew that she would never get back up again. "It really isn't here, is it?"

"Not the music box, ma'am," Bernard said. "It isn't. But that's what Mr. Pulcheck wanted to talk to you about. I'm sure of it."

"What could have been so important about it? A broken old music box." The disappointment of it all was a burden her heart could not quite undertake. It turned her sweaty and short of breath.

She swiped at a wet fringe of hair.

Hetty reached for the closest shelf and picked up a hand-mirror—the glass cloudy, the silver plate worn thin on the handle.

"This is marked," she told Bernard. "I don't have my glasses." She gulped, still struggling for air. "What does this label say?"

"It has a name on it, ma'am," Bernard said, inspecting it. "An owner's name."

Hetty's breathlessness dissolved into whispery laughter. "Of course he did," she said, clutching her chest. "Of course he would keep track. Just like he kept track of the broken music boxes at the shop. He knew exactly which item belonged to which person."

Hetty's laughter wound down. "I always wondered about that. About how he could justify keeping these things that meant noth-ing to him and everything to someone else. He was going to give it all back, wasn't he? At some point? When? At the right time? When would that be?”

Hetty glanced about the shelves. And she knew, now an old woman with so much of her life stripped away, how important a trinket could be. Some reminder of the past. Or of someone you had loved. Didn’t she feel that way about Gent’s music box? Hadn’t she just ached to wind that first box of his one more time, to find it not broken, but working, letting that music inside pull her back, like time had wheels and could take her somewhere else? Somewhere prettier, happier? Didn’t she think holding that music box would allow her to feel Gent beside her, to experience one more time a touch she would never have believed she would crave so badly?

Remorse crept along like a sunrise. What sort of woman had she become? Shouting at people and shooing them away from her home. That wasn’t who she’d ever been. Not who Gent had loved. What if he could see her now? And what of everyone’s memories? What had she done to those? The erasure of Gent’s kindness from the town’s mind—that had been her doing, had it not? Hadn’t she tainted everyone’s memories of the Bonwit house?

How bad she felt. Worse than losing was destroying something all on her own. And of all things—Gent’s memory. His kindness. She simply could not let that be colored by the way she had been behaving.

She could not let the town forgetting him be the last sentence in his story.

“Bernard,” she whispered. “Oh, Bernard. I’ve been so wrong. Will you help me?”

“Help you with what, ma’am?”

“Making amends,” she said. But she knew, rusty hinge that she was, that she would have to get going. “We have to begin tonight.” For Hetty Bonwit, the second hand did not have many ticks left in it.

"HE'S GOT TO LEARN that it's the kind ones who are always getting hurt." Or so Walter's mother was telling his father later that evening, the two of them off in the kitchen, discussing young Walter as though he were nothing more than a persistent problem—a thrashing, bucking ride they would just have to white-knuckle until it finally rattled off to a shuddery end.

They talked about him—or, more accurately, his mother talked about him, and his father listened, his silence being taken yet again as complete and total agreement. His mother paced, her large feet clunking out a drum beat on the kitchen floor as she laid out the details of the never-ending conundrum of their Walter in the same way she had talked about money the past few years, the pennies needing pinching and the dollars needing stretching. Walter was a bad situation that had been foisted on them, not unlike the Depression itself.

Walter stopped short in the front room before he made it to the kitchen entrance, his mouth dry and his heart beating that uncomfortable sort of hard that only accompanied the worst kind of nervous dread. He had come down wearing his shoes and holding the ad with the detail about the STA-KLEEN insole, having finally found the courage to tell his mother his shoes were too small.

But the serious way his parents were already talking about him kicked a familiar heavy stone into the pit of his stomach. So he stepped to the side, out of view of the doorway. He listened, his ears suddenly tuned into their conversation like the antenna on their Philco console radio.

"You should have *seen* him today when he came home," Walter's mother informed his father. "Big tears streaming down his face. Because Hetty *Bonwit* yelled at him."

"A regular melodrama!" his father teased. And then, before she could come back at him angrily: "Don't you suppose that what you see as a troublesome situation is actually a rather run-of-the-mill boyhood?"

Hope added still more speed to Walter's anxious heart. Was his father actually speaking up for him?

"Run of the mill!" his mother shouted, his father's suggestion lighting a regular fire in her. Through the crack in the door, Walter could see her shake her head until all her finger waves came loose around her jaw. "From the moment I first saw the baby with that little blue beanie on his head, I'd braced myself for scraped knees and bad marks in school and mischief. That's what a boy signaled, after all.

"And haven't I tolerated all the regular, expected bumps? Haven't I endured Walter's pertussis and his inability to memorize Civil War generals' names? Though the generals' names *still* astounds me. For heaven's sake—he only needed to remember them long enough to take the history test."

Walter frowned, finding himself confounded in return. Memorization wasn't like he was carrying a heavy box and only needed to get out the door. Memorization was the same whether you had to remember for a week or a year or the rest of your life.

"The one thing I can*not* endure, not one minute longer," Walter's mother informed his father, "the one thing I had not anticipated when I saw the blue beanie, is Walter's tender heart."

"Oh, you've said this before," his father argued. "I don't think it's a thing to be scrubbed out like grass stains."

"He gets his feelings hurt so easily!" his mother insisted. "By his schoolteachers telling him to pipe down or someone in his class telling him they can't come to his birthday party because their aunt's come to town. The world is constantly bumping into him, as the world is wont to do. But most people either kick back or manage to shrug it off. They look down at themselves days later and see the big giant bruise the world gave them, but suddenly, they can't remember where it came from. Walter? He gets mortal wounds. Stabs in the gut, each time—something he might never recover from."

Walter's mother began to bang dinner plates on the kitchen table. "That tender heart is about to snap me in two," she warned. And it was an intimidating sort of warning at that. A woman the size of a heavyweight prize fighter, Walter's mother had always been the muscle of the family. The woodchopper and the mechanic and the scolder and the bellower. His mother was the one who put her foot down—and a heavy, forceful foot it was.

"He's only bringing all this anguish on himself," she growled.

Walter was wounded by her words, even as the tiniest of voices inside him began to protest that this was all a bit like the giant ogre of a fairy tale demanding in a thundering voice that Walter needed to stop feeling *or else.*

How did someone simply stop feeling something? For no reason other than they wanted to? Who could really do that? Stop feeling affection for his best bud? Or stop being afraid? Wasn't his mother ever afraid? Didn't she know how hard that was? A feeling didn't exactly have a spigot. It plain wasn't turn-off-able.

"It's been somewhat excusable up until now, because he was a child," his mother went on. "But he's too *old* for this. I was younger than Walter when my father died, and we all went to work. All us girls. All five of us. Including me. All to help our mother. We did anything for a little money. Chop the neighbor's firewood. Paint their front porch. My sister Lilith had a job starting our neighbor's car, because she was afraid to do it herself. Lilith hand-cranked it for her. Every time she needed to drive somewhere. And the neighbor would pay her a penny."

"That was brought on by disaster, though," Walter's father pointed out.

"We were old enough and tough enough to step in. That's my point. What if Walter were drop-kicked into the world on his own? What would he do?"

"He has plenty of time—"

"What, to become a tenderhearted *man?*" Walter's mother said, disgust lacing her voice.

Somehow, that was worse? The reasons for this felt hazy to Walter. But for some reason, he instantly got an image in his head of the tramps who lived in the field behind the railroad depot.

"Really," his mother shouted at his father. "Crying! Because some senile old woman snapped at him."

"But why insist he come by the Bonwit home at all?" his father asked, his voice quiet and calm. It was the calmness that made Walter stop breathing a moment, his eyes fly open far wider. If Walter's mother was a fairy tale giant, his father was the beanstalk itself, slender and stoic. But here it was, again—an attempt to reason with her about Walter. "He could go the long way from the library or that lot where they all play ball when it's warm enough."

Walter's heart lurched inside his chest. *Yes!* Here it was. A solution. One that worked out in his favor.

"And delay supper till it's cold, I suppose," Walter's mother snapped. "What will you suggest next, that perhaps we let him go the long way to school as well, so that he's a good hour late each morning? That we spend the entirety of our lives sitting in this house waiting for him because he's got to go a mile out of his way every time? That's an easement out by the side of her property. It doesn't belong to her. And that's the shortest route between our neighborhood and everything he needs to get to. All the other children take it. They ignore her. Stick out their tongues and go on their way."

"And you would prefer that?"

Walter dared to smile, just a bit—to chuckle in a breathy, silent way. Had his father been a tenderheart just like him?

"It's normal," his mother insisted. "When you get hit, you're supposed to hit back. That's *normal.* Besides, what do you think is best—allowing him to chicken out? The easiest, quickest route for Walter is through that easement. The same route he has every right to use. Period."

"I suppose," his father sighed.

Those two softly-spoken words knocked down the fragile tower of Walter's hope.

Walter folded the ad for Ball-Band shoes and slipped it into his pocket. He couldn't talk to his mother about it now. He pulled his feet free of the shoes and carried them to the window seat in the front room, where he curled up into himself, hugging his knees.

He turned to the world on the opposite side of the window,

staring at the blackened street and the starry sky. His childish fantasies warmed him on that cold night—if only, he thought, he could switch places with the moon. The moon was so far away from other people who were always telling you that you were wrong or disappointing them or bothering or inconveniencing them. The moon was bright and important. And it was nothing but a head, completely removed from its troublesome heart.

As Walter pushed his face closer to the window pane and its frosty edges, another face jumped into the space between him and the moon. So close, it filled nearly the entire window.

It was a woman, Walter realized. An older woman, wrinkly not just around her eyes and mouth like his mother, but all over her face—tiny little hairline cracks, like his grandmother. But that skin also glowed. There was no other word for it. Glowed like some sort of celestial body, fallen down from the night sky. Glowed out from the folds of a black cloak, draped over the top of her head and covering her hair and casting shadows on her forehead.

She smiled at him.

Walter smiled back.

She winked.

Walter's head jutted back in surprise. Somehow, it seemed as though she knew he needed to play, to forget his shoes and the conversation continuing on in the kitchen.

He stuck his tongue out.

The woman tossed her head backward. Her mouth was open, and Walter could hear her laughter through the glass.

Somehow, in that moment, there was understanding between the two creatures: Walter and…who even *was* that? *What* was that? A stranger, a trespasser? Even a real woman? A figment? Another of Walter's fantasies, one of those daydreams that fueled him in secret, kept his tender heart pumping? Was this simply a dream about a little piece of kindness that he needed so desperately right then? The made-up image of a woman just as old as Hetty Bonwit, but completely different? Was this a fantasy? Was Walter making up the idea of Hetty's complete and total opposite? A person who didn't seem to think that sweetness was silly, or that tender hearts were weak or bothersome?

The woman's eyes twinkled as she made her own face at him, one that twisted her mouth and had her crossing her eyes.

Walter laughed, too.

When she uncrossed her eyes and looked right at him, Walter swore her bright blue eyes were no longer just twinkling playfully but sparking, with white bursts of light. Not like a frayed electrical cord, though. Not like something damaged. More like something magical. Her eyes sparked like shooting stars. Like something you could wish on and feel certain your wish would come true.

Walter felt a kinship with the woman he had never seen before. He was closer to that woman than he had ever been to another living being—maybe even closer than he was to Petey. Because in that moment, they understood one another. In a single moment, they were friends. And it was good to be Walter Drummond.

But then the woman's eyes shifted from his face to a spot behind Walter's shoulder. The smile vanished and her cheeks sagged. An expression of fear flashed, and the woman darted away.

Walter turned, finding his mother in the center of their front room, her fists on her large round hips and a scowl on her face.

She dropped her hands and clomped straight for the door. Each step shook the floor the same way a wolf shook a kill in its mouth.

She raced outside, down the front steps. A moment later she returned.

"Walter," she thundered. "At what point do you stop staring at an intruder and start taking action?"

Intruder? She hadn't even attempted to come inside. Or threatened Walter. "She was smiling at me," was all Walter could manage. The words were still there in his mouth when his mother's cactus of an expression started making shame crawl across Walter, prickly and dangerous.

"Your tender heart will be the ruin of us all," she growled.

Walter hugged himself tighter. The magic of the moment was gone.

"We'll make our trip downtown on Saturday," his mother proclaimed. "First thing in the morning."

Had they already planned such an outing? Walter didn't think they had. Then again—did she already know about the shoes? Was it possible? Had she seen him hobbling into the house that afternoon? Was that why they were going downtown? Two full days left. And on one of them—tomorrow, Thanksgiving—he wouldn't have to walk to school in his shoes. He could stomach the idea of dealing with the shoes on Friday only, then heading downtown to get new ones on Saturday. He felt a smile coming on—nearly as joyful as the one the woman in the window had worn.

"We're going to talk to Charlie Barister about this. He's always easy to find downtown on Saturday. An *intruder* in the *neighborhood*," his mother said. So there it was—nothing about Walter's shoes at all.

His disappointment was never given the opportunity to take root, though—not with this news about the two of them having to report the woman.

"Officer Barister? Why? She wasn't doing anything," Walter pleaded.

"We're going, and that's final." When she looked him directly in his eyes, though, Walter saw his mother begin to soften. And in the softness, he also thought he saw her acknowledge that what she wanted was hard on him. "It's not just for us, Walter. It's for the whole neighborhood. It's such hard times. People like her—tramps and vagabonds and—who knows what else. They're out looking to take. And we have to be on our toes, looking to protect. That's just how things are. Now, please put your shoes away where they belong and come down to dinner. Hurry. It's getting cold."

Officer Barister, though…he was a tough cop. Everybody knew that. One of those by-the-book guys. Walter could not wipe the smiling woman's kind face from his mind. Before he could stop it, Walter's tender heart was cracking all over again.

7.

Saturday

CHARLIE—*OFFICER BARISTER,* BECAUSE no one would dare call him by his first name anymore—drove along the fringes of the town of Sullivan encased in shiny newness. His patrol car, a 1938 Chevy complete with giant painted badges on the doors and shiny, unscratched, fat black fenders, had only last month arrived equipped with a fancy shortwave. The people of Sullivan didn't have much those days (in fact, hard times had been beating at their doors so long, it had started to feel like a permanent state), and so it seemed even more important to protect what little they had left. Officer Barister was their investment, one that would be with them for a long time to come. He was still a young man, but settled, and there to stay for good. His wife and son and their house over on Pearl Street were proof of that.

When the three of them were downtown, passersby tossed them the kind of knowing smiles that said they remembered it, the speedy feeling of those early family years, when they could hardly get used to one picture before everything changed completely. One day you think you'll never be done boiling bottles and the very next you're watching the same baby ride a bike all on his own, down the street, out of sight.

Charlie's current family portrait, the picture that surrounded him at home, was one of marveling at the sparkly icicles that hung from the edges of their gutters and cheering and pointing at the approach of the rumbling milk truck.

Charlie himself felt a little like squealing and pointing—not at any loud, speeding vehicle, but at the calendar. It was nearly December. And for the first time in his son's three years, he would be able to find true joy and anticipation in Christmas. Oh, he'd been a little aware last year. But this year? He'd be able to easily shred tissue-wrapped packages and know there was a gift inside. To tug on Santa's beard when he wandered from the edge of the parade. Why, Tom would *talk* to Santa that year. Nod insistently when Santa asked if he'd been a good boy.

Yes, Tom was that beautiful age, the age when he could fully understand the holiday but there would be no disappointment, no gift asked for beyond the family's means. He was still so young, anything would delight Tom. Peppermint candy or a shiny penny or a teddy bear stitched out of his outgrown clothes.

It was going to be a year of joy. Of learning how to believe. A year in which a little plastic candle was actually a promise. When stars twinkled in a way that told Tom they all knew his name and would carry his wishes straight to the North Pole.

Charlie hummed "Jingle Bells" to himself as he tried to figure out where they might start that holiday season. Breakfast with Santa at the café? That was a definite, of course. But should they really *start* with such a big event, or would it be better to work up to it?

How hard it would be to decide—but the difficulty made Charlie's heart skip about joyfully, playing a game of hopscotch in his chest. Sullivan had always been a Currier and Ives painting of a town. Pink cheeks in the cold and snowball fights and the sound of children's laughter. Spiced cider and chocolate pots in the front room and Christmas cards arriving in giant piles, so many you could string them up all over the house—down the mantel or over arched entryways. Some years, when he was a boy, Charlie and his mother had even cut them into ornaments for whatever small tree they had brought in from a neighbor's field. A few still owned family land back then, though not much farming was done out that way anymore, not even when he was a boy. Once December arrived, all you had to do was ring a doorbell to get immediate permission to go cut the tree of your choice *and when you're done be sure to come back, sit by my fire here and warm your fingers.*

And then it hit Charlie, the perfect place to start his holiday celebrations with Tom—the pond. Of course! He hadn't ice skated in years, not since those early Christmases when he still dreamed of cast iron toys beneath the tree. But it was magical, the feel of the wind in your hair as you sped across old man Pendleton's pond. Laughter was constant out there, so much of it that it began to sound a little like the chatter of birds. He remembered how he and the other boys had taken turns holding up their principal, Mrs. Winton, because she was never steady on her skates. And there were races, too, when the pond cleared, the boys challenging one another.

Tom was too small for ice skates, but Charlie was sure he had a pair somewhere. He could hold Tom in his arms as he skated. He could hear Tom now, squealing as they made their way around the far edge of the pond. In his head, already, it was the sound of pure joy.

His insides hummed, vibrating even more than his Chevy as he drew closer to old man Pendleton's place. If only he could see the pond from the road. He craned his neck, a smile spreading through his cheeks when he saw the figure at the end of the lane. He rolled down the window, the winter air swirling a fresh chill across his face. "Got your skates with you?" he called.

A heavyset woman glanced behind her, stopping her waddle through the early snow. She changed direction, tugging her galoshes free, one after the other, making her way toward Charlie's patrol car. She shoved her face in through his open window, her expression one of teasing familiarity. "You think the force bought you this fancy car just so you could go skating all day, Charlie?"

"What about you?" he asked Ida. "Going to join the kids this afternoon yourself? I remember trying to get you out there on the ice with us when I was a boy. But you were always so busy with the Pendletons—"

"Oh, the holidays are still full of parties for the Pendletons. *Good night*," the longtime family cook swore with a shake of her head.

"Don't tell me you don't join in on the parties anymore."

"I'm too old for such foolishness," Ida declared. "By the time I get all the treats made, I'm ready for bed. Sometimes, after the last of it's done, I don't even bother to stop to see what little extra thing the Pendletons put in my stocking."

It was good to be so close to Ida, this remnant of his childhood.

"I *might* stay up if we could have another night at Frankie's like we used to," Ida admitted, nudging him playfully.

Immediately, Charlie's smile disappeared. Why would she even mention it? The speakeasy that had once opened up after dark, accessible to anyone who had been able to beat the secret knock on the back-alley door of Frankie's diner. *Why?* Why would she bring that up? Especially to him?

"Ol' Frankie," Ida said, her voice dripping with fondness, "she sure had her own rules. And who was ever going to argue with *her?*"

Yes—who? Six feet tall and four feet wide and known to keep a derringer in her stockings like a regular gun moll on the silver screen. Who would ever dare challenge that? Frankie was the one woman in all of Sullivan who had been able to intimidate Charlie himself, even as she'd offered him a friendly hand. She had always given Charlie the feeling of being near an animal far bigger than you. One that was mostly docile but also a threat, because everyone knew animals always had the ability to turn on you in a moment. In Frankie's after dark, it was her rules or else. One of her rules was that Charlie Barister was a-ok. A young cop who understood the gray areas and could keep a secret. *One of us*, that was how she'd put it. The good guy who could look the other way. Another rule was that Ida was welcome to take a seat right there, right at the bar. Even though Jim Crow demanded she be in a separate spot everywhere else.

And so he and Ida had sat side-by-side, drinking Frankie's bathtub gin. They had listened to music played by real-life sweethearts—Chester on trumpet and Dorothy the chanteuse with the gardenia tucked behind her ear. Charlie'd Lindy Hopped and he'd flirted and he'd kissed a few girls in the darkest back corners and he'd convinced himself that Frankie's rules were the only rules that mattered, because it was the only place that made sense. There, he and Ida (that kind face from his boyhood) could drink from the same bottle, and Frankie could finally make decent money—enough to keep her day-time diner ("Home of the 5¢ steak!") going, and they could all dance and feel as though they had a place where they belonged.

Before he could stop himself, a part of Charlie started missing that. And as soon as he dared to miss it, the missing taunted him with the story of how it all had ended. There it was—the Christmas Eve disaster that had put an end to Frankie's for good—hitting him with a fresh wave of regret. He wanted to get back to his original reason for stopping, back to dreams for pleasing his son, but those dreams had tarnished a little now.

"My Tom's getting to be old enough," Charlie said, his smile now feeling dishonest to him. "For—for the holiday. I was thinking of bringing him by here. It's been unusually cold. So I figured everyone's started showing up. To—to skate, I mean," he added, wondering why she was frowning at him in that way.

"Now, Charlie, you know better than that. I thought you were playing with me, asking if I was going skating."

"Better than what?"

"We haven't had a soul skating out here for years. Only thing that pond is good for these days is making old Ida here have to get more exercise than she wants because she has to take the long way around. Bernard made me promise long ago I wouldn't take my winter shortcut straight across. We all found out the hard way that ice can't always be trusted. Especially early on in the winter."

Ida raised her head and glanced up and down the street. "Where is that Bernard, anyway? He's always showing up in the morn-ing, right about the time I need to make my way around that pond. You know last week, he even shoveled a path for me in the snow? You haven't seen him, have you?"

Charlie shook his head, still thinking of the pond.

"Maybe it's that old Model T of his. Been trying to fix it. Maybe it up and went kaput on him for good."

"The pond," Charlie croaked.

"What about the pond?"

"Why doesn't anyone skate on it anymore?"

"Why? Nobody been out there since that boy died. You didn't forget that, surely. What was his name? The one who fell through and drowned."

Charlie *had* forgotten. Completely. How could he? Another town tragedy, one that had played out long before the speakeasy shootout. So many years. How old had Charlie been when it had happened? A boy, it seemed. Still. How did a person lose track of such a thing? Charlie hadn't simply outgrown the skating. It had been stripped from him. Deemed dangerous. How could that have slipped his mind? How could he have rewritten it to be something else?

Ida patted his hand. "Never you fear. You're having a hard time finding things for your boy. I know. Not too many places offering goodies for the young'uns. No breakfast with Santa this year."

"No breakfast?"

"Nobody can afford to take their whole family out to eat, Charlie. You see that every day. Sounds like the powers that be even decided to abandon the parade and the tree lighting this year. Shame. They all need Christmas."

"But that can't be," Charlie protested. "Surely, that's not—"

"You bring that little boy of yours by, and I'll be sure to whip him up something special. Maybe some homemade marshmallows. Toast 'em up real nice. Get him all sticky and happy myself."

She waved and headed off once again, her galoshes slopping through the snow. Off to the kitchen door, to cook yet again for the

Pendletons. Another day, another batch of meals that would be devoured in mere minutes, over and done with to clean up in order to come back tomorrow and begin again.

Charlie felt unnerved watching her walk away. His excitement for the coming season had dimmed. The magic of it had taken a hit. That couldn't be true, what she said. Could it? That Sullivan wasn't going to have much of a Christmas season? After all, even in hard times, there was still shiny newness. Right? Look at where Charlie was sitting. His brand-new Chevy.

He cleared his throat. Shouted, "You have a good day, I–"

But she was too far away to hear. He wanted her to turn around, to come back. To tell him that things weren't so far from where he had left them. That it was fine and not foolish at all to have put his own childhood away in a drawer and expect it to still be there, like an heirloom, to pass down to his boy.

He *needed* those things. Tom did. Skating and sweetness and places like the pond—they weren't frivolous. They were the most important blocks to build on. Because what Tom wound up thinking of the world while he was growing up—didn't that determine what kind of man he would become? Wouldn't it matter if he thought kindness and sweetness were the engines of the world? Wouldn't that change how he moved in it?

Charlie's heart ached at the possibility that more things could be gone, things he had counted on for Tom. But how could that be? Childhood was childhood.

He steered toward Main Street, the wheel pressing painfully against a cut on the palm of his hand. He hadn't even realized it was there until a moment ago. But at a red light, he looked, and there it was, the scab thin and fresh. Where had he gotten it? On the razor that morning while he shaved?

He gripped the wheel tighter, even though it hurt. And he steered down the strip toward the biggest, busiest stores. Surely signs of the holiday would have popped up along the town square. Signs he had not noticed yesterday because he had not yet been looking for them.

But as he snaked down the street, he saw no signs of Christmas. Only a few desperate sale signs—some old enough to have warped in a long-gone rain—and a rare "Help Wanted" sign at the bakery. No red and green. No stars. No peppermint stripes.

Everything was looking trampled on. A bit brown. Worn thin. This, too, seemed a tragedy. One like the pond—or the speakeasy. Yet another sad ongoing tale that Charlie had shoved aside, refused to look at square in the eye.

Why had he done that?

"B1, B1," the shortwave squawked.

Charlie—Officer Barister—lifted the receiver. He cleared his throat. "B1 here. What are your details?"

"Possible break-in at 304 Main."

"Three-oh-four, did you say?" Charlie asked, his voice cracking at the end.

"Confirm, B1," came the voice through the shortwave.

Charlie's slumped deep into the front seat.

304. The address of Frankie's old speakeasy.

8.

THE BUS CARRYING WALTER and his mother jerked and sputtered through the streets, heading downtown.

"Well, I told my Walter," Mrs. Drummond announced to the rest of the passengers, "I told him, Walter, we can*not* give this woman license to come in and wreak *havoc* on our neighborhood." She turned and glanced at herself in the bus window. Used the side of her fist to wipe away some steam. Leaned into her reflection. Adjusted the tiny hat on her head—the one she wore each Sunday, with cherries embroidered into the mesh across the front.

She straightened her back, proud to announce her goal. "After everything we've all been through, we simply cannot allow it. It's for all of us, of course."

Everything, of course, meant the recent years that had left them all feeling completely out of control. Spiraling, chasing after money or work or security. Things that had felt so solid in the previous decade, like steel. Those days, nothing felt solid anymore. Living on sand did something to a person. It had done something to Mrs. Drummond. She had learned about sand once before, as a girl, when her father had died. But she had considered it her rough patch—over and done with. Her own adulthood needn't be spoiled by such hardship.

And then of course, the Depression hit. Here she was, and it was rough all over again.

But this? An intruder into her neighborhood? Why, that was one wolf she could keep from coming back to her door.

"Yes, I said to Walter, 'Walter, we *must go tell Officer Barister.*'"

"Those are plans best kept to oneself, I believe," Irving Rosenbaum grumbled from his own seat two rows up, rustling his morning paper.

Mrs. Drummond straightened her back, shifting her shoulders. "Maybe if *I* owned a jewelry store, I wouldn't have as many worries," she said.

"Oh, yes you would," Irving answered without lifting his head. "And that's why you would wind up having to add the word 'Optician' to the front of your store. To make ends meet. Or at least try to. Folks can go without bracelets, but they can't go without eyeglasses."

The bus rolled to a stop, pausing to let passengers on and off. Bernard Whitaker boarded, having to stoop his tall frame in order to get on the bus. Everyone began to squirm, inching themselves into the middles or aisles of their seats, attempting to discourage him from sitting with them. He was that nasty Hetty Bonwit's housekeeper. They pitied him, having to deal with her all day. But they resented him a bit for allowing her to get so out of hand. Shouting at their children and carrying on so. He was the one who could have convinced her it was unnecessary.

Petey's dad stepped on board wearing coveralls—the kind janitors at the hospital wore, even though he owned the town's only funeral home. Irving Rosenbaum finally lifted his head from his paper long enough to look behind his shoulder. The half of his face that was visible clearly wore something of a smug look. *See?* that look said. *Everyone has problems. So many, in fact, that they have to resort to the horse track two towns over. And then they go so much farther into debt, they spend their Saturdays cleaning hospital rooms while their son is left holding down the fort at the funeral parlor.*

It was, in fact, not unusual for so much to be communicated with such a brief look in a small town.

But Mrs. Drummond's eyes had already fallen on the Rossis, boarding on this stop as well.

Yes, Elizabeth and her mother had just started walking down that metal aisle when Mrs. Drummond patted the seat in front of her. "Ladies," she said, as an invitation.

"Did Walter tell your little girl about our intruder?" Mrs. Drummond pressed as they settled into their seats. After all, Elizabeth and Walter were quite close in age. The kind of close that made them friendly with one another—able to share an eye-roll at an overly-loud parent, for example.

Elizabeth swallowed a giggle at Walter's face and turned back around to face forward.

"Intruder?" Mrs. Rossi asked, clutching the top of her coat.

"*Gossip*," Irving Rosenbaum blurted. "Nothing but gossip," as he folded his paper under his arm and rose from his seat, clomping down the aisle.

As the door shut behind him and the bus started back up, Elizabeth glanced behind her yet again, to look at Walter. Right then, at that moment, they were two elementary-school-aged children, Walter in too-tight shoes and Band-Aids, and Elizabeth in an old dress of her mother's. It had been taken in, but she was still swimming in it, and could only hope the coat covered most of that up. Forty years from that moment, Walter would be walking down the sidewalks of Sullivan, Missouri in a three-piece suit, the chain of an old-fashioned pocket watch catching the sun. And Elizabeth would approach him, in heels, her blond hair twisted into an updo, her mouth and nails painted up red. They would greet each other warmly, and Elizabeth would leave behind the smell of her signature Cashmere Bouquet powder.

Forty years from this moment, he would be a banker and she the owner of the swankiest women's clothing store in all of Southwest Missouri. They would be regulars at Ruby's Place, the supper club that eventually would take over the space that had once been home to Frankie's old speakeasy. And they would become themselves two necessary ingredients in the cocktail of magic that would be rumored to exist right there at Ruby's.

Walter would become a stronger ingredient than Elizabeth, perhaps. After all, there *would* be a reason why Hetty Bonwit would find herself sitting outside of Ruby's Place on a Christmas Eve, thinking of Walter as she was bombarded by questions from a newspaperman.

Right then, though, long before even the idea of Ruby's Place existed, they were two powerless kids in clothing that did not fit and that they did not want to be wearing. They did not want to be thinking about the fact that it was nearly December, and Christmas was coming, and there was nothing they could really hope to receive—or buy, not for their families, not in any way that would make any difference.

Elizabeth looked at Walter, right there, on that bus, and Walter shrugged. "She didn't intrude," he assured her, trying to privately correct his mother's tirade about the stranger he had seen at the window.

"What did she do, then?" Mrs. Rossi wanted to know.

"She was *trying* to get in," Mrs. Drummond said.

"Maybe she was only hungry," Mrs. Rossi suggested.

Elizabeth leaned back. Shielding her mouth from her mother, she whispered to Walter, "They carved a picture of a cat into our fence."

"Who?" Walter hissed.

"The tramps. From the railroad depot. It's code. 'A kind-hearted woman lives here.'"

"Kind—?" Walter asked, his heart keeping time, now, to the spinning of the bus wheels.

Elizabeth nodded. "Because Mother feeds them."

"And they never hurt me," Mrs. Rossi added, showing Elizabeth she could hear her every word.

Elizabeth flinched and retreated into herself. She and Walter exchanged a brief sympathetic look. Forty years from then, they would be the ones calling the shots in town. Making bigger decisions. They would not be biting their tongues.

"Don't hurt you?" Mrs. Drummond asked. "When you go to your cupboard and it's bare, doesn't that hurt the family?"

"If I needed help, they would help me."

Mrs. Drummond snorted with disbelief. "Have they ever returned any of your favors once? Have they ever come back to pay you for your kindness when they could?"

Mrs. Rossi didn't respond.

"And you think they'd help if you needed it," Mrs. Drummond grumbled, amazed at Mrs. Rossi's naiveté. She whacked Walter with her elbow. "A tenderheart," she grumbled. "With nothing in her cupboard because she's given it to bums."

But Walter felt invigorated by the way his mother had tossed out the term. A tenderheart! Right there! Out in the world! They existed. And they married and loved and maintained daily routines. Maybe, just maybe, tenderhearts had a bit more to offer than his mother would have him believe.

When Elizabeth dared to glance his way—one last time—he grinned at her. He had a plan. He was not going to help his mother give up the beautiful stranger whose smile had made him happy. Not to Charlie Barister. He would not allow her to be arrested or sent packing out of town. He was going to help her.

He did not know it right then, but this was perhaps one of the biggest moments of his life. Right here, sitting on this bus. This seemingly small decision of his—to protect this strange woman—would be a reason why so many wonderful things could take place in Sullivan's future. His decision was the foundation for his work at the bank and for Elizabeth being able to own her dress shop and even for Sullivan's greatest landmark—Ruby's Place. Yes, Walter's decision right here, at this moment in time, was turning him into a magical ingredient.

It would take decades for them to know it.

Right then, on the bus, all Walter had was a plan.

And a spark of courage.

9.

BERNARD DIDN'T MIND SO much that no one wanted to talk to him on the bus. In all honesty, he wasn't much in the mood for talking. He had a pursuit of his own now, one started by Hetty a mere three nights ago. Why, this mission of Hetty's was as grand and honorable as any the US military had undertaken! Or so Bernard's hopeful dreams had him believing. Yes, Bernard was helping Hetty bring to life the idea that had come to her in the storage room: Return the worthless trinkets left behind by carriage house guests. Trinkets saved by Gent. Trinkets whose only value resided in the hearts of the original owners. Hetty was energized—even happy. It was like the old Hetty had come back to him.

They had already seen success, but in order to keep going and not lose their momentum, Bernard needed to get to Grady's Garage. It was the only place that might have what he needed for the Model T. He couldn't go on driving around after dark in a vehicle that coughed and sputtered, threatening to die and making the kind of noise that would draw attention, invite people to look too long, give Hetty away.

Already, the clank and rattle of that old car had made lights turn on in front windows, front doors flop open, shouts hit the night sky. *What's going on out here? What's the big idea?* Bernard and Hetty had nearly been found out a couple of times. A person couldn't keep tempting fate.

Bernard was in a hurry. But he decided to get off at a stop that was still several blocks from the square—another twenty minutes or so out of his way on foot.

He was halfway to the Pendleton pond when he caught Ida waving to him.

"What're you doing out this way, Bernard?" she asked. "I didn't think you worked here today. In fact, I didn't think you were scheduled to work until the spring kicked in again."

"You say this every time you see me," Bernard told her, taking her arm and attempting to lead her toward the sprawling four-story house, the biggest in all of Sullivan. "If I'm anywhere near the Pendleton place, I'm going to make it a point to come out here to help you."

"Shoot. You think I don't make it on the days you're *not* here? I've taken this very same path every morning since that sun's been rising. I know exactly where the edge of that pond is. I know how to avoid falling in."

"You can let up on pretending you don't like it," Bernard said as the two headed toward the kitchen door, the one Ida had been coming and going from for the last five decades. "You and I both know you're far colder than you usually get on your morning walk. You've been standing out here waiting for me, haven't you?"

"Ah, Bernard," Ida said. But it wasn't a scold.

Bernard grinned despite himself.

"Won't be long before you'll have this place looking all bright and cheerful again," Ida said. "All those flowers you plant. Sure do love what you can do with that green thumb of yours."

Bernard had always assumed that being good at something meant you would also enjoy it. Gent certainly had. But Bernard did not exactly enjoy all the pruning and clipping and planting of bulbs. It seemed to him a flower that bloomed only a couple of days was a poor payment for the amount of work that went into getting the flower to open.

He had thought, during the times he had been feeling a bit down, that it was also a metaphor for life.

Not that day, though. That day, he had a whistle dancing from the edge of his lips.

"Snow's deeper than I thought it'd be out here," he mused. "I'll be by tomorrow to shovel a better path for you."

"Oh, Bernard, you are too kind to your old Ida."

But that didn't seem the right word. Not to Bernard. Kindness was frivolous, wasn't it? Unexpected? It was a batch of cookies all for you, out of nowhere, *just because*. Shoveling a path was simply something that needed to be done. It wasn't something extra.

"You ever gonna tell me what you really want to tell me?"

Bernard offered a crooked grin. "You know me too well."

"So spill it."

"I shouldn't tell you. That's the problem."

"We'll chip away at it, then. What's bringing you out this way?" Ida asked as the snow crunched under their feet. "We'll start there."

"Grady's Garage. I need some spark plugs for Hetty's Model T."

"*Hetty's* Model T?" Ida repeated. "Not Mrs. Bonwit's? I don't think I've ever heard you call it that. Does *Hetty* suddenly have a purpose for the old Tin Lizzie?"

Bernard smiled. Offered only the teensiest of nods.

"Come on, Bernard. Out with it. You know nobody keeps confidence quite like old Ida."

"She's returning all the trinkets."

"What do you mean, trinkets?"

"The items everyone left behind. In exchange for help."

"I didn't know she still had any of them."

"Gent kept it all. Cataloged, even. So she knows who owns what. And now, she's got it in her head to return it all!" He grinned in the way of little boys—the smile overtaking his entire face. "We've been out the last few nights. Started already. But the car needs spark plugs to run smoother, I think, so I'm—"

Ida stopped walking. "Why does she want to do that, all of a sudden?"

"It's Christmas. It's for Christmas."

Ida stared at him, her dark eyes full of knowing. "That sounds a little like a woman's last wish."

"No," Bernard protested. "It's not that at all. It's a renewal! It's like Gent's back in the house. She's smiling and humming. You should see her. It's like the old days all over again. When there were still guests in the carriage house to take care of. It's been years since we had anyone, as you know. Because everyone was aware the Bonwits had started to struggle. Even before Gent died. *Everyone* was struggling, of course. Even—"

"How long's she been doing this?"

"Started earlier this week. The day before Thanksgiving."

"Why are you going out at night? Why's it all hush-hush?"

"That's because she doesn't want anyone to know it's her. You see, her thinking is—she has to keep it anonymous, because so many people have bad feelings associated with her now. Because of how she's been chasing everyone away. She wants this to be something magical and inexplicable, something they'll remember always. Something—" He couldn't say the rest. Because maybe Ida really was right about Hetty's why—even a little.

"Something wonderful left behind," Ida finished.

Bernard shook this away, admitting, "I'm afraid she might not have kept her promise to me. You see, I made her give me her word that she would stay in the house while I came downtown today to get the spark plugs. After I fixed the car, we would go out again later tonight."

"Now, why would she up and leave during the day, Bernard, if she wants to keep it all secret? Anonymous, like you said?"

"Because." Bernard took a deep breath, hating that he was getting so close to Ida's reasoning again. "She's in a hurry to get it all done."

When Ida pursed her lips and put her hands on her hips, he insisted, "Because Christmas is getting so close. She wants it done in time for Christmas. That's the hurry." At least, he hoped it was the only hurry. "But now she thinks she has more strength than she does. She might try to come see you."

"Me?"

"She has something Frankie gave to Gent in exchange for one of Gent's loans."

"Never a loan with Gent. It was give."

"That it was. Frankie used the money Gent gave to buy the liquor to start her speakeasy."

"I'd assumed as much," Ida admitted.

"You know where Frankie is now, don't you?"

Ida only stared at him.

"You've never lied to me before."

"Ain't going to now."

"So you do know."

"I might."

"Hetty wants to bring it to you. This thing of Frankie's. Wants it so much, I'm afraid the promise she made to me to stay put at home might very well be about as empty as the Bonwit bank account."

Ida chortled. The way to Ida's heart, Bernard knew, was through her laughter.

"Hetty might be out here today," Bernard went on.

"Where?"

"The woods," Bernard said, nodding once to the trees along the Pendleton place.

"Good night! You can't be serious."

"It would be the shortcut between the Bonwit house and the Pendleton place. I knew you'd keep an eye out for her if I told you. You'd make sure she was all right."

"Good *night*," Ida said again as she stared off into the distance, her eyes pointed at the woods.

Bernard guided her the rest of the way to the Pendleton back door. But neither one of them had anything left to say. Only the weight of worry to share.

"You ought to make a wish while you're here," Ida said, pointing to the snow-covered pond. "Before you head on your way. Best time of year for wishes to come true."

"A wish?" Bernard repeated.

"Why not? Charlie was talking that old pond up before you got here. Wasn't all that big or special of a pond. Still isn't. But he was acting like it was the greatest thing ever in town. I can kind of ignore it most times, but days like today, when somebody's been talking about it—makes me think there's some reason it's still here. Something good keeps it from drying up. Sure would be nice if Sullivan had its own wishing pond."

"My throwing a wish into it isn't going to make it a wishing pond, though, right?" Bernard asked, playing along. "It has to be a wishing pond first."

"That can't be right," Ida said. "Nobody knows how to be anything until you tell them. Nobody would ever have sense enough to put clothes on, half the time, unless you told them they had to. Nobody would even get thoughts in their head until you showed them how to speak. So maybe if we all started going out there and making wishes on that pond, it might get the idea in its head to be something other than a run-down, muddy, deep puddle."

It was a good idea. Bernard liked it. Even though it was a bit silly.

When he left Ida, he started back toward the street. He need-ed to hurry on to the garage. Carbon buildup, he'd decided. That was what was making that old car sputter. New spark plugs, that was the solution.

As he walked, though, he turned Ida's word over in his hand, smooth as river rock. *Wishes*, she'd said. He had plenty of wishes. The wish to do this thing for Hetty. And another—a selfish wish. The wish to find that old music box. He didn't tell Ida, but he and Hetty had spent part of the night before—in-between trinket-runs—searching the speakeasy for the old box. Searching again after so much time had flickered something back to life in him—hope, it seemed. Hope that he could still make good on his promise to Gent.

Yes, hope. What a glorious little bit of alchemy. A mere drop of hope had turned the lead of Bernard's guilt for losing the box into the gold of a soon-to-be-fulfilled promise. He *would* get that music box to the bank. Bernard knew it. He would. He had just been delayed a little, that was all.

Suddenly, his feet were pointing toward the old pond. It was nearly December, after all. The season for wishing—and for the inexplicable magic of making wishes come true—was officially underway.

10.

JUST AS BERNARD HAD feared, Hetty was, at that moment, in the woods between her home and the Pendleton place. Ambling along, fighting her cloak, which was old, and made of what felt like the scratchiest wool.

The brittle tips of branches kept getting stuck in the thick, textured fabric, snapping off in the cold. As Hetty ambled forward, she reached up, feeling the cloak now full of tiny bits of winter trees and bushes. She had to be a sight—surely she looked as though she'd been living right there in the woods for years, existing in some lean-to propped up against an Ozarks hillside. She tried to avoid the path of an incoming branch, but wound up scraping the opposite side of her face against a different tree. The surprise of the scratch sent her stumbling, her balance easily lost.

She planted her cane deep in the ground as a way to steady herself.

She paused for a moment, putting her hand on a low branch.

Through the stretched-thin leather of her glove, she could feel the cold. The chill told her the tree was coated in ice. Had there been freezing rain last night? When she and Bernard were out, had she felt sharp, frozen prickles dancing on her cheeks? It seemed she'd asked herself this question already that morning. Even her thoughts repeated themselves, like footsteps she was tracing.

It was time to rest. She dusted snow off the flat surface of a tree trunk. It was almost like the tree had been cut just for her, a little chair. She sat, even though she knew that being immobile would let her bad feelings catch up to her again—the ones that had found her when she'd broken her promise to Bernard and raced outside of her house.

She let go of the cloak. Just a little bit, relaxing her grip. But the wind chewed at her fingers, even through the gloves, so she slid her hands inside the wool folds, searching for warmth.

If only the town could see me now, she thought. But then again, they had. She'd worried that the town would easily recognize her during her night outings—Bernard driving her out to individual addresses, and Hetty racing up to the back door to hand over the long-lost items. But they hadn't. Not yet. Probably wouldn't ever. How funny it was that people only knew you if you were in the right context, wearing the right clothes, standing at the proper address. Anymore, the only context folks in Sullivan knew Hetty Bonwit by was the one where she was a cranky old woman, shaking her fists, mad as a junkyard dog.

Anything else, and they refused to even consider it could be her.

Winter cardinals flittered about near Hetty. She loved the woods. She loved the trees. It made her think of her father and his lumber.

She opened her eyes, staring out at the quiet, snowy woods. It felt so good to sit. But she couldn't rest long. Not if she thought she could beat Bernard back home. Yes, she would have to get going.

She put her hands beside her on the tree stump, ready to push herself off.

She had work to do.

75

11.

"ON MY WAY," CHARLIE said and replaced his shortwave in the dash compartment. Only after he started driving in the direction of the old speakeasy did the rest of the words sink in: *possible break-in?* What did that mean? How could someone not be certain that something was stolen?

Two blocks north, Charlie slipped his patrol car into a parking space outside Puddin's restaurant and killed the engine. He walked to the door, situated below the gold-tone "304" adhered to the brick. But he found the entrance to the establishment locked. Cupping his hands, he tried to look through the large plate glass front window. But a giant *Out of Business* sign and the darkened interior obscured everything.

"Herman?" Charlie called. He knocked.

When no one answered, he made a face. The same kind of face his wife made when their cat brought home one of his "presents," as they referred to them—a recently-killed bird or rodent. His wife was fine with knowing that the cat killed innocent creatures every day. But she didn't want to have to see the reality of it, have to dispose of it, know she was partly responsible by merely owning the cat in the first place.

Charlie would have to circle around to the alley.

He walked slowly, his footsteps adding a kind of syncopated rhythm to the pulse in his ears. It was a familiar path, but one he hadn't taken in the last seven years—certainly not on police business. Nerves took hold, hitting him like the strongest drink. The closer he got to Herman's back door, the looser and floppier the muscles in his arms and legs felt. If someone were to tackle him, he would fumble. He knew that. And he hated it. Fumbling and not being ready, that was how people got hurt.

At the back door, Charlie raised his fist. Before he could stop himself, he pounded out an almost-forgotten rhythm. The secret knock that had once gotten him into Frankie's speakeasy.

Herman answered.

His face, as usual, glistened in the morning sun. Charlie'd never seen a man sweat so much. Herman sweated through the winter. He sweated through shirts and sweaters and was always loosening his tie and stripping off his suit jacket, and there they'd be, giant sweat stains all over his shirts. Starch wilting faster than a telegram racing across the wires. At first, Charlie had thought that Herman used far too much pomade, but later realized even his hair glistened with sweat. It was getting worse. Charlie wondered if sweat in the winter would make icicles hang off Herman's earlobes.

"Got a call about a break-in?" Charlie greeted. All business.

Herman opened the door wide enough for Charlie to walk through. As the door swung, Charlie's eyes moved against his better judgment, landing on the section of the door he'd been trying to avoid. Bullet holes near the bottom, beside the hinge. In the last seven years, the holes had yet to be filled. They had weathered, the splintered wood graying and softening.

Charlie didn't want to go inside. He stood rooted in the same spot in the alley as he pulled a notebook out of his back pocket. "If there were no injuries or destruction to property, I can jot down your missing items here. Got another call to respond to," he lied.

"Destruction?" Herman wiggled his lips, letting his shiny face catch the light. "Not quite. But—you gotta see this for yourself."

Charlie gulped. His head swam. But he forced himself to step through the door.

This was it. The back part of the old restaurant that had once been home to a speakeasy. During the daylight hours, Frankie ran a respectable diner. The same diner her father had run. Homemade biscuits and steak with cream gravy, fresh apple pie. After dark, she locked the front door, and she turned out the lights. From the street, it appeared the diner was locked up tight for the night. This room in the back—shut off by a thick wall so that the lights and noise would remain hidden from out front—was then open for business.

Charlie hadn't been in this side of the building in ages. Not since the speakeasy days.

And it was—good God, he had expected an empty room, but so many of Frankie's things still remained.

The large oak bar—where *had* Frankie gotten it?—stood poised at the front of the room. It was a beautiful bar, its railing or-nately carved. Life-sized flowers and giant acanthus leaves and scroll work swirled along the edges. A leaded-glass mirror still hung behind it. The room in the reflection was filled with the same tables. Ivory keys on the piano in the back, long quiet, waited beneath yellowing sheet music, still propped on the music stand.

Frankie's speakeasy had never look rough. It had never been sleazy or unsavory. It was lovely. After a while, it felt as though it was *secret* only because the regulars wanted to keep it to themselves, for fear of having it be overrun with too many people. Not because it was something you needed to hide from authorities.

But Sullivan did hide it. All of them. Even Charlie. He had kept the secret.

Oh, he was spinning now. He put his hand on the edge of the bar. He tilted his head down, and he saw it, that knock in the wooden panel down near his feet. He had been sitting right here as a young cop when the handcuffs had fallen from his pocket. His sweetheart had left him, and he'd had more than his usual.

His handprints were all over this old speakeasy.

"Officer?" Herman asked, "you okay?"

Charlie nodded, afraid to speak. He took in deep breaths with closed eyes, trying to settle his stomach.

When he opened his eyes again, there he was, in the mirror. His reflection younger. He had not yet married or had Tom. There, in the mirror, memory and reality collided.

Memory came out on top.

He could feel the regulars all around him now. The room behind him clamored, full of people shouting and carrying on. So many of them, it was hard to believe they could actually move enough to dance.

"The usual?" a familiar voice shouted into his ear.

Frankie. Standing right there at his side. She asked him a second time, louder, obviously assuming that he could not hear her. He almost didn't. Not with Dorothy belting out "Puttin' On the Ritz," her voice as rich as her charmeuse gown. She leaned over the piano, her gardenia falling out from behind her ear. Her husband's trumpet soared. Dancing feet stomped. Ida swayed back and forth on her stool.

Frankie brought him a drink—something clear in a fancy glass. "Listen, I've been meaning to ask you something," she said. "Where *were* you that Christmas Eve?"

"Where was I?" Charlie croaked.

"Yeah. Where were you. Christmas Eve. 1931. The first Christmas Eve you *didn't* spend here after I opened. What gives?"

"I—I had a Christmas party."

"Christmas party, my foot. You let things spiral, you know. Everything. Way out of hand."

"What was I supposed to do, though? Report you?"

"Heck, you coulda gone after Maxwell. You knew how he was out trying to sell that homemade concoction. Made with that big old still out there at his farm. That man was peddling the stuff everywhere. I would have been a real coup. But I said no to the fool. I already had my supply. Wasn't going to upset the good thing I had going. You had to know he'd try to get even."

"I couldn't know he'd call the station."

"Hogwash. What kind of *policeman* are you?"

"Was I," Charlie tried to correct. "I was young. I couldn't risk him giving up information on you when he got hauled in."

Frankie scoffed. "You weren't that young. You came here. Through the *alley* door. Every night after knocking off. You knew Maxwell would be out for revenge. Maxwell Ross never let a single thing go. Not ever. And instead of figuring something—anything—out, you ignored it. You let Maxwell fester. Get mad enough to call my place in. On *Christmas Eve*, no less. Who knew the police could mobilize so fast?"

"I didn't know. I was—"

"—at a party. How convenient. You weren't here for the

shootout. Right here. Right on this floor. Because your own precinct contacted the state police for backup. Potential for organized crime, they said. They burst in here with their guns drawn. And my guests here, they reacted. Without thought. A few drew their own weapons. Blood was shed here. On Christmas Eve.

"Poor Dorothy got arrested. I went on the run. You had some impossible choices, maybe. So I might give you that. Rock and a hard place. Fine. But you made the wrong choice, Charlie. And you weren't even here the night it all happened. You, who sat right here, guilty as the rest of us, and never had to pay. I paid. You think I wanted to leave my business behind? My own father's restaurant. Do you ever wonder what happened to me?"

"All the time," Charlie murmured.

"Charlie? What do you mean? All the what time what?"

It wasn't Frankie that Charlie was staring at. It was Herman's sweaty face twisted up in confusion. The room around them was empty.

That is, empty of people.

But it was, in fact, still completely full of furniture. Not exactly the way it had been when Frankie's speakeasy was open. Large boxes were everywhere. Many of the chairs had been stacked on tables. The piano really was still there, though. And the bar.

"I was using this area for storage," Herman explained. "This stuff—it's the stuff from Frankie's, you know—I had some of it out front, where I was serving folks in my restaurant. I'd been warned not to. Because of—well. You know."

Charlie did know. He knew too well. He nodded, hoping that Herman wouldn't continue. But he did.

"The Christmas Eve shootout," Herman went on. "The night they busted Frankie's speakeasy. What was that—five, six years ago?"

"Seven," Charlie said, the shame of his past still raw. If he'd done his job—been a real cop and not everyone's buddy—busted Maxwell and his still—blood would never have been shed on Christmas Eve. Maybe Maxwell *would* have snitched on Frankie, like Charlie had suspected he would back then. Snitched as soon as he got arrested—*if I'm going down, so will she.* But even if that had happened, Dorothy probably never would have been arrested. Frankie might have served time, but it would have been over by then because even Prohibition was over. Frankie would never have had to leave town, gone on the run. She would have been home.

By that point, Frankie would maybe be running an honest club, even. Maybe Dorothy would be singing in it.

Nothing would have been as bad as a Christmas Eve shootout. People getting hurt. He really had made the wrong decision. He had always known that.

"Charlie?"

He flinched, turned back toward Herman, the only proprietor who had ignored the cautions—*place is tainted*, everyone said. *Cursed. And even if it isn't really, folks seem to think it is. No one will go inside, not anymore. Why would you ever try to open a business there?*

"Y—yes," Charlie managed, swallowing hard. Herman had gone out of business, like everyone predicted. At a time when he might never recover. How could he? What did you do, when times were hard everywhere, and you needed to start fresh? There was no such thing. Not then—maybe, for all Charlie knew, not ever.

"I thought everybody was nuts telling me I shouldn't move into Frankie's old place," Herman said. "I got such a deal. I couldn't resist. Frankie—after she went on the run, nobody could track down the deed. Nowhere in any of Frankie's important papers, and nowhere at the bank."

"I remember," Charlie murmured.

"How do you misplace that? A deed!" Herman held his hands out from his sides, sweat cascading down his face. "So the building was considered—"

"—abandoned," Charlie finished. "And the local government, believing it to be an ownerless property, took it over. Leased it out."

"Turns out, there really are bad feelings about this place," Herman said. "Tarnished, like everybody tried to tell me. But I wouldn't listen. I had such great hopes for this place—I got the best Ozark Pudding. I know that sounds like bragging. But it's true—who doesn't like apples and nuts, right? And my recipe's got a cornmeal crust and a molasses drizzle on top. Couple secret ingredients, too. I thought for sure my little bit of sweetness would overpower any sour left over from Frankie. No matter what I did, though…" He shook his head. "Guess the investors who steered clear of this old place were right." Herman wiped his sweat-slick forehead.

Charlie tried not to show any expression. "Is anything missing?" he asked, attempting to redirect their conversation.

"I'm not sure."

"Not sure?"

"I can't figure it out. Strangest thing. When I came in this morning, I thought it looked different. Boxes out of place, that sort of thing. And then I thought—*Well, maybe I did it.* In the hustle of closing up shop. But as I kept looking around, I *knew* it wasn't me. I know I didn't leave some of these things this way. The place looks rifled through. Doesn't it? That's why I wanted you to take a look. Tell me I'm not crazy."

Charlie glanced about. "Without knowing exactly what it looked like before—" he started. But stopped when he noticed the pulled-open box tops. In one area of the floor, his toe knocked against a large meat fork with long tines that clearly could have been used to tug a nailed-down wooden lid free.

"But I can't for the life of me figure out if anything's been taken," Herman went on. "I can't think of a single thing that's missing. But why go through this stuff and not take anything?"

Charlie frowned. It *was* awfully strange. He had to give Herman that.

"The back door," Charlie said.

"Nope. No sign anything was jimmied or broken. No real evidence of a break-in at all." Herman shrugged. "Anyway, I almost didn't report it. But I got to thinking—I'm not too far from the railroad."

Charlie grunted. The Hooverville out behind the depot. That was what Herman was alluding to. The group of tents and shacks put up by the tramps who had gotten off the train and found no greater opportunities in Sullivan than they had anywhere else. That camp had become the blame for any rotten turn of events in Sullivan: *Must've been somebody from the railroad.* Charlie had come to suspect that the poorest souls out there would soon be blamed for too much rain, the buckling streets, a sweetheart's wayward eye.

"Now, the door thing's still a mystery. How somebody might be getting in here, I don't know. But I do wonder if somebody's getting in here at night," Herman went on. "Maybe to sleep. Getting pretty cold at night now. Far too cold for their camp out there, I'd say."

Charlie's scowl deepened. He didn't like where this was going.

"What if they do something like try to light a fire in here? I'm just renting—but I can't have this place burn down, officer. Not on my watch. I can't be blamed for it. I'll never get out from under that one."

Sweat dripped from Herman's chin. "I wish I'd never set foot in this place."

He looked right at Charlie and really laid it on thick with a, "You respect the law, Officer Barister. I know you won't stand for anything bad to happen."

The truth was, Charlie *had* let something bad happen. Right here. A Christmas Eve raid. The past swirled as it had a moment ago—not the past he wanted to revisit and share with his son, but the one he'd wanted so desperately to move on from. It was back, his biggest mistake, the icy cold teeth of his bad decision chewing on him as it pulled him farther down, threatening to drown him.

Yes, prices had been paid for Charlie ignoring the speakeasy. Frankie had paid. Dorothy had paid. The regulars who had been shot had paid. Even Herman was paying, because no one could get past the bad feelings of that Christmas Eve shootout.

Charlie? He was still a cop. Same as always.

He was a different cop now, he reminded himself. A man who respected the law, just as Herman said. He had never been accused of being a traitor by anyone. He had used the second chance to change his ways. No more being anyone's best bud. No more looking the other way. A line had been drawn between citizens and officer. Years late, maybe, but—

Suddenly, Charlie's new leaf didn't feel like enough. He had this strange, overwhelming sensation that he needed to make amends.

With who, though? Frankie? She was long gone.

With Sullivan, he told himself.

Charlie shook Herman's hand and made a few promises—on the lookout, come back tonight, that sort of thing. Herman led him back outside—through the front door, that time.

As Charlie started for his patrol car, a woman's voice called out to him. There they were—Mrs. Drummond and her son, Walter, heading right for him. Mrs. Drummond raised her hand over her head and waved, indicating she had been the one to call him. She had that look on her face—the one she got when she expected him to take care of something *on the double*. As she stomped, she rustled the cherries on her hat.

Charlie groaned, dreading what she was about to bring his way, not suspecting at that moment that Mrs. Drummond and Walter were about to bring him the very thing he wanted most—the chance to finally, finally make things right.

12.

"MY SON HAS SOMETHING to tell you," Mrs. Drummond announced.

Walter shifted back and forth uncomfortably, refusing to look Charlie in the eye.

"Officer Barister, we need to talk to you about an *incident* in our *neighborhood*—" Mrs. Drummond said, unable to stomach Walter's silence, unwilling to coax him gently into the tale. Taking over the responsibility for telling the entire story herself.

She was such a large, imposing woman. Her frame was almost an identical match for Frankie's. Yet another reason why Charlie didn't want to deal with her. Not today. And especially not over yet another petty grievance.

"Oh, now, Mrs. Drummond, we've discussed this before," Charlie said, already wrung-out by the morning. He didn't think he could stomach another chapter in the trivial, longstanding fight between the Drummonds and their neighbor. "I know Hetty Bonwit isn't easy to deal with. But the—"

Mrs. Drummond shook her head until Charlie thought the cherries attached to the mesh of her too-small hat might fall off. "It's not her," she insisted. "It's someone else. She—I don't know. She's a bit of a ghost."

"A ghost!" Herman bellowed from behind Charlie's shoulder.

Charlie shot him a warning look to take a step back. But Herman didn't notice. He wagged a thumb at Mrs. Drummond. "Maybe that's what I got at my place, too, eh, officer?"

Charlie cringed; no one hated not being taken utterly seriously more than Mrs. Drummond. He had learned that in previous run-ins. On cue, she pursed her lips and bristled.

At her side, though, Walter squirmed, his chin tucked into his chest and his hands stuffed into his pockets. He looked ready to burst, pushing at the seams of his clothes. But there was another sort of pushing. Charlie could feel it. Something inside of him.

"Something wrong, son?" he asked him.

Walter shook his head insistently. He had decided on the bus that he would not talk to Charlie. He had hoped to go unnoticed—most times, adults did just that. Refused to even notice a child. Being ignored—now, that turned a person into a *real* ghost. For once, that was exactly what Walter hoped to be. But here Officer Barister was, waiting for Walter to respond.

Walter didn't like Charlie Barister. Everything about him looked as precise as the corner of a building. Those weren't just pleats in his pants. That wasn't just an ironed collar. Those were edges of bricks. Officer Barister wasn't ever going to understand about the stranger. Not like Walter understood.

"*Well,*" Mrs. Drummond huffed. "It's so incredibly hard to describe her. She comes around at night ducking in and out of the houses in the neighborhood. First our home and then, on Thanksgiving night, a few more neighbors saw her. I think she might be looking for a place to get in."

"Might be the same person," Herman said, tugging on Charlie's arm.

"What person?" Mrs. Drummond wanted to know.

"I got somebody who broke into the back of this place," Herman said, his sweat kicking in yet again.

"Now, there's no indication this is the same—" Charlie started.

"Did she steal anything?" Mrs. Drummond wanted to know.

"Well, not yet," Herman said.

"*Herman*," Charlie scolded.

Walter recoiled at the severity in his voice.

"It's only a matter of time," Mrs. Drummond said. "Someone that needy might *become* dangerous. A regular intruder and thief."

"Officer Barister, are you listening to this?" Herman asked.

"Please," Charlie said, holding his hands out.

"Did you say you saw her yourself?" Herman asked Mrs. Drummond.

Buoyed by his interest, Mrs. Drummond threw her shoulders back and took in a breath. "It was quite difficult," she said. "It *was* after dark. And she was wearing a black cloak."

"You don't say!"

"Herman," Charlie scolded, but neither he nor Mrs. Drummond was listening.

"*Yes*," Mrs. Drummond said, pursing her lips and nodding in a somewhat over-exaggerated way. She knew that Herman was not leading her on or mocking her or feigning interest. He really did want to know. He was almost frothing at the mouth for more information.

"Her face," Herman said, too interested even to so much as shiver standing there in the December chill without a coat. "What about her face? Was she old? Young? Someone you'd seen before?"

"I didn't see. Walter did," Mrs. Drummond said, pushing Walter a step closer to the two men.

Charlie looked down at Walter. A boy only a handful of years away from his own son's age. He tried to imagine how Tom would feel, all these adults hovering overhead. Demanding he come clean. He tried to put on a gentle air. "What did she look like?" Charlie wanted to know. "You can tell us. It's okay, son."

Walter tucked himself farther down, like a hermit crab trying to cram himself into a space too small. He wanted them all to go away. "She wasn't like that at all," he murmured. "She was kind."

"Kind!" Mrs. Drummond barked, shaking her head. "Can you believe him?"

Charlie raised a hand again, more insistently this time, attempting to quiet Mrs. Drummond. He didn't want to discourage Walter from giving a full description. "She might very well be kind," he agreed. "It might be that we need to help *her*."

Mrs. Drummond sucked in a deep breath and shook her head, but Walter seemed to soften a bit at this notion.

"Can you give me a description?" Charlie asked.

"She…she was…she looked a little like. Well. Like the face in the moon."

"Oh, *Walter*," his mother scolded.

But he only tucked himself even deeper into his coat.

The heat of Mrs. Drummond's anger brought a flush to her cheeks that rivaled the cherries dancing along her forehead. Here she was, having come all the way downtown, dragging Walter and enduring that infernal bus ride. And now, after all of that, he was going to refuse. Act like an insolent child. He was *going* to help, her anger decided. He was going to help whether he liked it or not. "I volunteer Walter," she announced.

Walter could not get his mouth open to protest as his mother pushed him forward.

"He'll help you," Mrs. Drummond announced.

"H—how?" Walter managed.

"You will help Officer Barister track this woman down. You'll know if he's got the right person. After all, you're the one who's seen her." Mrs. Drummond fished a dime from her purse. "For the phone if you need it." She snapped her purse shut. "But I trust you won't. You're with a police officer. The safest place in the world to be. I'll see you boys tonight. Dinner is at seven, Walter. I'll expect you home at that time."

None of the three boys standing there thought Mrs. Drummond could in any way be serious. Surely, Charlie thought, she was only trying to put the fear into Walter. Make him burst out with the truth before she disappeared around the corner.

When that didn't happen, Charlie told himself he was making this up. Just like the vision of Frankie or the sight of the speakeasy. This was surely something that he was envisioning. Something his guilty mind was drumming into existence.

Only—there she went, walking down the street. There she went, boarding yet another bus. The one that would take her home.

And there Walter still stood, growing red and recoiling right at Charlie's side.

Herman broke the silence. "Quite a partner you got there," he wheezed, laughter shooting out between bouts of a smoker's cough. He shook his sweaty face and started back toward his out-of-business restaurant.

"Bet he'll be just the person to get to the bottom of this here secret. A stranger skulking about Sullivan," Herman called out, before disappearing back inside.

That word—that *secret*—bounced down every single bone in Charlie's spine. Secrets were dangerous, or so he had learned. He had kept a secret in Sullivan before—the secret of the speakeasy. This time, though, Charlie didn't even know what the secret was. And that made him nervous. So nervous, in fact, that he could feel a sweat not unlike Herman's begin to break out across his forehead.

A *SECRET.* CHARLIE FELT it against his skin, prickling and chafing and making him itch. A strange woman. Darting about at night.

He glanced down at Walter, who glanced back up at him. Charlie's eyes admitted that he knew exactly where he needed to go, where he might begin to tug at the root of this secret. But in his eyes was also the admission that he knew he could never take Walter there.

Still, he smiled. Just as he hoped someone else might someday smile at his own Tom.

In return, Walter's eyes asked how this could have possibly happened—how he could have wound up like this, discarded at Charlie's feet. His eyes apologized.

"Come on," Charlie said, patting Walter's shoulder. "I really do need some help with this one."

But Walter's eyes shifted, right then, to become a warning. He would not hand her over. He would not help Charlie find the woman who had tapped on his window and teased him so playfully and happily, smiling at him through the glass.

The moon. She looked like the face in the moon.

"What'd you mean by that, anyway?" Charlie asked. "How could someone have looked like the face in the moon? I mean, now that it's just us. You don't have to worry about what your mom would think."

Walter cringed. He didn't want to think of his mother. But he didn't want to talk to Charlie, either. He saw Officer Barister, right then, as an extension of his mother. They all were, all the grown-ups. Except for maybe kind-hearted Mrs. Rossi…and that strange woman who had made him happy with her smile. She understood things, the way she teased him. He would not let them come destroy her. He would *not*.

Charlie sighed. "Going to be like that, is it? All right, you can come with me to the newsstand. Your mother won't be home for a while, anyway. Not if she's taking the bus. No sense in driving you straight home."

"Why the newsstand?" Walter asked, following along behind him down the sidewalk.

"Well, it *is* where you get the headlines. Right?"

"Not your headlines. Not the ones you need," Walter said. If getting to the bottom of where to find the woman was the issue, anyway.

"Folks are *always* chatty at the newsstand," Charlie told him.

But when they arrived, and Charlie tipped his hat, the entire gathering there at the newsstand flinched. They scooted to one side or another, seeking a little extra space between themselves and the cop.

Charlie felt a silent bricking up of the space between himself and those who had stopped to glance through Sullivan's daily paper. A quick look at the Classifieds to see who might be hiring for day jobs.

"Hey, there," Charlie sang out, smiling.

No one responded.

Walter sucked his top lip into his mouth, trying to hide how much this pleased him.

Things had been different when Charlie visited the newsstand in the time before, as he often thought of it. Before the trouble at Frankie's—and before that trouble had made him a real cop. He'd stopped chewing gum like a kid. Leaning against streetlights and flirting with girls. Talking big at the barber shop. The trouble at Frankie's was what made him finally fasten that button on the top of his uniform shirt. Made the other officers at the precinct stop referring to him as the young'un.

Charlie glanced behind his shoulder, to make sure Walter was still nearby.

Walter tugged his hand away from his mouth, straightened up, and tried to look serious.

"So," Charlie said. "Got a case. A report of some break-ins. Looking for some additional information."

There seemed to be a rush, then, to plunk a coin down on the newsstand and take the paper off *in such a hurry, can't talk now.*

"Wait," Charlie tried. "Wait." But the rushing continued, people slipping away from him like so much melted snow between his fingers.

"Just a moment of your time, that's all," Charlie assured the three still left, the ones who had formed the back of the line, who had waited for everyone else to pat down their pockets and finally find the money for their papers.

A scowl etched itself into Walter's face. These three, he thought, would help Charlie. Mostly because they were in the business of helping people: Rose the switchboard operator at the phone company. James Wilmington who owned the Sullivan Drug Store. And the Westbrook woman, the one who was such a good friend of Ida's, the one who had worked out there at the Pendleton place—doing what? Walter wasn't sure. One of those straightening-up jobs.

When it was your job to do what people requested—whether it was connecting a call or serving a vanilla phosphate or straightening up the Pendletons' front parlor—it became something of a habit. You *always* did what people asked you to do, whether it was share your last cup of sugar or offer up every last drop of information to a police officer.

At the newsstand counter, Charlie announced, "I'm looking for a woman," which made Walter take a step closer, his hands out, like he could somehow stop all this from happening.

"A woman we suspect of breaking into a business right here on Main," Charlie went on.

Rose reached up to touch the necklace at the base of her throat. A strange necklace—one made out of a single pearl on a kite string.

Walter took a step toward them, thinking maybe he could put himself between Charlie and whatever Rose might say. Instead of taking a bullet, he would absorb whatever tip she might have to give. But Charlie flicked a warning look over his shoulder.

"A woman in a black cloak," Charlie added.

At the mention of the cloak, James placed a hand on his coat pocket.

Charlie and Walter did not know that James had a letter opener in his pocket, once owned by an uncle. And that Rose's single pearl had belonged to her grandmother. Or that family lore had swirled around those objects, because the owners had missed them but also because they had said something magical had happened when those objects had been handed over. Their fortunes had been found.

No one at the stand—not one of them—knew *this*, but the silence surrounding the details had simply been the way of the Bonwit charity. No one had ever spoken of it directly, in concrete terms. Because they had promised Gent. But the stories wanted out. It was the way of story, after all. Stories clawed at the inside of a person, scratching and whining and begging to be seen. So the stories had finally been told, over time, but in a veiled way. Metaphors and mystery filled the strange family tales, handed down from one generation to the next. The Bonwits' charity had always worn a black cloak, it seemed.

But now pieces were being returned, strangely, at night. Handed over by a woman no one recognized. Pressed into their palms. The items were all still as worthless as ever. But with them came slices of yesterday. More than they were getting old trinkets, they were getting back people they had lost. Here it was, a letter opener so worn from an uncle's hand that touching it took James back to being a boy and feeling his tiny hand engulfed by his uncle's fingers as he led him across the street. Here was a pearl from Rose's grandmother, a final pearl that she had had to surrender to Gent after all the other pearls had been sold. She had hoped to hang on to that last one, even though it was misshapen and flawed. It was all she'd had in the world. Or so she had hinted, giving Rose a string of her own pearls when she was only twelve. *It can save you like it saved me*, her grandmother had said, with tears in her eyes. And now, here, on a silly string around Rose's neck, was her grandmother. And all the dreams she'd had for Rose. After all this time. Touching that pearl was like being with her grandmother all over again.

The Westbrook woman started to back away while Charlie zeroed in on James.

Walter had always liked the Westbrook woman. She still liked to dance and twirl beneath falling snowflakes or make snow angels right there on a city sidewalk. A child at heart, most called her, if they were trying to be kind about it.

Mrs. Drummond was invariably among those shaking their heads at her in a more disapproving manner. She'd often grabbed Walter's hand and tugged him in the opposite direction, insisting it was what happened to silly tenderhearts. Always before, his mother's words had made Walter pity the Westbrook woman. But right then, he liked her. He especially liked the way she had never grown as stiff and severe as the rest of the world.

Charlie kept on, trying to grill James and Rose for information. But Walter slinked away, following the Westbrook woman. "Ma'am?" he hissed. "Ma'am!"

Westbrook turned, looking him square in the eye. Few adults did that. Looked right at him in a way that said they saw him as a human being and not as an animal that needed to be given commands.

"You saw her. Didn't you?" Walter whispered. "It's okay. I saw her, too."

Westbrook's eyes swelled. "What did she leave you?"

"Leave me?"

"She always leaves something," Westbrook insisted. "Everyone's getting something. Things that belonged to your family. Things they had given up. Things that mattered. Still matter. For some reason, they're all showing back up. No one can explain it. Look what she brought me." She pulled a strange-looking shell with teeth out of her pocketbook. "It goes in your hair, see?" she asked, showing him how the shell was not a real shell at all, but a comb made of abalone. It shone iridescent in the sun, almost like the sheen on top of a puddle of oil.

"It used to belong to my mother. I don't know how she found it. The woman in the cloak, I mean. I'm going to send it to my niece. She's a big-time ballerina up in New York. She can wear it in her hair when she dances, see?" Westbrook held the comb to the crown of her head, rose up to her tiptoes, and skittered off toward the post office.

"Wait," Walter hissed. "Wait."

But the Westbrook woman couldn't be bothered, not with his questions, not when she had a gift to send by air mail, straight to glittering New York City.

Had that woman been to Walter's house to give them something? What? Had his mother scared the woman away before she could do it? Would she return and try a second time? What if Charlie got to her before that happened?

Now, Walter's heart was pulled in two directions: keep Charlie from finding the woman, or help him so that Walter could himself get close to her long enough to find out the true reason for her visit.

Then again, he wondered, was that last option even truly a possibility?

Charlie clomped to Walter's side. "You have any luck?" he asked, his voice laced with disappointment.

Walter glanced behind him, finding the newsstand empty except for the solitary worker there behind the counter.

So they hadn't talked to Charlie. Rose and James had gotten away from him without telling him anything. Others were protecting the woman just like Walter was.

"What did Miss Westbrook tell you?" Charlie persisted, nodding once in the direction the woman had gone.

Walter shrugged.

That shrug sent ripples scattering across Charlie's face. There was such sadness and frustration in it that Walter felt his stupid heart wanting to reach out to him. To make him feel better. "Nobody wants to talk to the principal," he offered.

"Say again?" Charlie asked, positioning himself in front of Walter, towering.

"It's—why—no one—talked," Walter said, already regretting the fact that he'd offered Charlie some help.

It was such an insightful thing to say that Charlie felt rattled.

"Why'd you even want to be a policeman, anyway?" Walter grumbled. "So you could be mean to people?"

"Mean?" Charlie repeated. "I'm not mean. I'm following the rules. I—" But there it was. He hadn't looked at it in so long, but it was still with him, even after all that time: the reason he became a cop.

"Officer Talbot," he said. "Frank. Frank Talbot."

"What about him?" Walter asked.

"He was my reason."

"Was he in your family or something?"

"No—he." Charlie paused, shook his head. Decided to go ahead and tell Walter the truth. "He caught me stealing."

"What'd you steal?"

"A little cast iron toy. A policeman. If you can believe it."

"A *toy?*"

"I was about your age. Cast iron toys were very important to me at the time."

"And then what, he hauled you in or something?"

"No—he didn't. He could have. He—paid for the toy. With his own money."

Walter grunted. Charlie could hear a, *Too bad you're not as nice as that guy* in the grunt.

"Then I had to pay *him* back. Officer Talbot. I had to work off my debt. He had me working at the precinct—taking out trash, shining up everybody's shoes, that sort of thing."

Charlie hadn't thought of him in so long. Why hadn't he? "We got close. After a while, I sort of idolized him. He was everything to me back then. All I wanted was to be like him."

"And now you are," Walter said.

Was he? Charlie remembered Officer Talbot's ways—how he always had a new knock-knock joke. How he liked baseball and licorice and seemed like the biggest kid. Charlie was a different sort of officer. He was now, anyway.

"You know, Walt," Charlie started, trying to shake off this bit about Talbot. "I would never arrest someone who's not doing anything wrong."

"She's *not* doing anything wrong," Walter protested. "She's not that way."

"Okay, then what if she does need help?" Charlie asked. "What if she's trying to get in someplace like Herman's restaurant to get warm?"

Walter shook his head. "I don't believe you," he dared to say.

But Charlie could not rid himself of the feeling that Westbrook had talked to Walter. Charlie was hit by an overwhelming desire to squeeze the boy, get that information out. But the feeling faded when it occurred to him that maybe Walter was right—that bit about the principal. And maybe, by leaving Walter with him, Mrs. Drummond had actually given Charlie a prize—something that really would help him uncover Sullivan's secret.

Charlie took in a breath and looked Walter over, head to toe. And his eyes settled hard on the toe. The bulging seams. The way Walter tilted both feet to the side, as though to throw off the pressure of his full body weight. The way he kept lifting up first one foot and then another, as though to give each one a break.

It was time, Charlie decided, to strike a deal. "If you're going to truly be my partner for the day, you have to have compensation."

"Say what?"

"Paid. You have to get paid."

"Okay." Walter got a little shiny at this, despite himself.

"But I don't pay in cash. I'll only pay in shoes."

Walter's eyes shot straight up to him—round, hopeful. Like a dog with the smell of bacon in his nose. But a dog who also knew he had to put down his one and only bone in order to get it.

"And what do I have to do?" Walter asked.

"You have to come with me somewhere to do an interview or two. And you have to tell me everything you find out."

Walter asked himself what kind of boy he was going to be. A traitor? Someone who would throw someone good to the wolves to save himself?

But his feet started throbbing all over again. And before he could stop himself, he was nodding. "Yes," he said. "I'll do it."

"MORNING, MISS," CAME A singsong call down the street.

Elizabeth Rossi stopped so suddenly her wagon smashed against the backs of her legs. Empty, the wagon didn't stop as easily as it did when it was bogged down by some sort of heavy load.

"Excuse me," he went on, "but I am an attorney for the Bonwit family."

Elizabeth's eyes darted back and forth across the street, hoping for an adult to come outside, ask what this strange man wanted with a little girl. Surely someone needed to take out the garbage or call their dog home. Where could the postman be?

"I have been attempting to contact Mrs. Bonwit for quite some time."

Elizabeth did not care. She needed to get home. Her mother had left the whole house in her care, and had rushed off to Edna Lightfoot's home to help with the extra laundry she took in.

And here Elizabeth was, only seconds ago feeling so very proud of herself. Here she was, having just returned the draperies her mother had mended for Mrs. Kowalski, the ones that had been singed by the embers from her fireplace. Here she was, her wagon now empty and the payment—ten whole dimes, so many shiny coins to keep track of—was jingling in the little drawstring coin purse around her wrist.

She had succeeded in doing this thing for her mother—bringing Mrs. Kowalski the mending job and carrying back the money. At least, she had almost succeeded. She needed to get home. She needed to get the money inside the house, place it on the kitchen table. She needed to get dinner started. She had promised her mother she would do that, too, while she was working at Lightfoot's.

Elizabeth did not need an obstacle like this.

"I once knew Gent Bonwit," the man announced. He was an odd looking fellow, with both greasy locks and a large bald spot. His suit did not fit properly, and he had an air of desperation that made Elizabeth incredibly uncomfortable. The world was a different place—far more unsettling—when you still had to look up to it. When nearly nothing was at your eye-level. And to now have this strange man in front of Elizabeth…her eyes darted about again. Where was her savior? Anytime one of the children tried to pick on another at the playground, a teacher was always nearby to swoop in and save the day.

Where was her playground teacher now?

"I apologize. My name is Arthur. Arthur K. Pulcheck. Esquire."

As though Elizabeth had any way of knowing what *esquire* meant.

"I left a note for Mrs. Bonwit. Dropped it through the slot in her front door. If you are a family acquaintance of the Bonwits, might you please let them know that the note is there? The Bonwit cats have a tendency to be a bit—" Mr. Pulcheck raised up both his hands and scratched at the air, pantomiming cat claws.

That was all Elizabeth needed. She took off running, the wagon rattling and clanging behind her. Stupid Mrs. Kowalski. Why had she had such enormous drapes—drapes that could only be carried in the wagon? If Elizabeth hadn't had that silly Radio Flyer, she really *could* have been flying. Running far faster than she was.

She could hear him calling after her. She wasn't sure if it was an apology or another appeal.

She didn't turn around to find out.

Elizabeth raced block after block, the cold burning her lungs. She clambered up her front steps and fought the folds of her dress to get the key out. She unlocked her door and jumped over the threshold and slammed the front door shut again.

She retrieved the step stool from the kitchen and used it to look through the peephole.

Mr. Pulcheck, it seemed, had not followed her.

Now, in the cool calm of her home, Elizabeth seemed to remember the look on his face as she'd taken off—embarrassment and sorriness and regret. She hadn't wanted to make him feel that way. She'd only wanted to be home.

She hurried to the kitchen, where she would have to light the gas stove in order to warm dinner—leftover cornbread and beans. She was still shaky, though, and had to work to remember the steps her mother had given her.

"Turn on gas flow," she recited, moving the knob. Then the hard part. The matches. She wound up dropping the Diamond box on the floor three times in her attempt to strike one. She held her breath, her fingers trembling as she grew closer to the gas stream. In a puff and a whoosh, the burner ignited. Elizabeth squealed as she adjusted the flame.

There. She'd done it. She smiled, the feelings of success returning to her again. She gathered up the navy bean pot from the ice box and placed it on the burner. And then she sat at the kitchen table, counting her dimes. All ten.

She was a very grown-up girl at that moment.

But the feeling, yet again, was only temporary.

In a few hours, the outside world would come knocking again.

And Elizabeth would be tossed upside-down.

15.

CHARLIE DROVE TO THE Hooverville out behind the railroad. That was what the men at the barbershop and the hardware store—the newspaper rattlers—called the encampment, bitterly. Similar camps had popped up all over the country, all of them blamed on the previous president.

The romantic version of such camps—the version that might make it onto the cover of sheet music—portrayed something of an outdoor hotel under the stars. Where people came only for a short time before moving on again. Getting right back on the rails.

The reality was something harsher and harder. Bleak and scraggly. Dirty canvas tents and rancid smells in the smoke of campfires. Icicles in socks and frostbite and empty stomachs. This encampment had been created by men who had once believed that something would be different in another city. But every city had been hit by the same fists. Here, tired men saw their hope turn brittle. They lost momentum. They stayed longer than they'd ever intended. By then, though, in December, the population was far thinner than it had been in the fall. The freeze had pushed them back onto the rails.

Charlie paused after killing the engine. Here, it could feel like life was a single train track, and once a body got derailed, there was no correcting it. What might happen to Tom if he ever got pushed off his tracks by the oncoming disasters of the world? What if Charlie wasn't around when it happened?

He looked over at Walter, in his too-small everything. Was he actually here, at the Sullivan Hooverville, with a ten-year-old? Had he really forced the child into this, bribing him with the shoes he needed? Was he really so desperate to undo his own mistake and give a Currier and Ives painting of a Christmas to his son that he was maybe even endangering someone else's son?

Mrs. Drummond left him with you, Charlie reminded himself. She wanted him to do just this—use Walter to help find the woman. A stranger, skulking through neighborhoods at night.

Walter sat, staring back at him until it became clear that he was waiting for Charlie to make a move before popping his door.

The two edged closer to the camp. One of the few remaining men—this one sitting at an open fire in front of his tent—stopped stirring whatever it was he was making to eye Charlie suspiciously.

Charlie smiled as he made his way still closer, frozen grass crunching a bit beneath his shoes. Somehow, it seemed colder out here, the wind slicing straight through Charlie's uniform coat. He knew it felt even colder to Walter, his clothes too thin for the weather and his young skin too thin for the harsh realities that played out here behind the depot.

Charlie had forgotten his gloves at the precinct, and he hated having to pull his hand from the warmth of his pocket. But he did just the same, offering it to the man to shake. "Officer Barister," he said, introducing himself.

The man turned his head slightly, looking at Charlie from the side of his eye. Charlie wondered if he'd had eyeglasses that he'd lost somewhere along the way and was trying to get a better look at him. He thought about saying something about his lost gloves, like somehow that could bridge the gap between the two of them. Like somehow, they were one and the same in terms of discomfort. And he hated himself instantly for thinking it.

Charlie let the man stare, though, doing everything he could not to let his own eyes linger too long on the rough, overgrown hair and beard, the threadbare coat and the chapped skin on his hands, the dirty nails and cracked bottom lip, the weariness in his expression.

And he refused to put his hand down. He continued to offer it, so long that the warmth of his pocket completely left and the cold began to sting against the cut on his palm.

Charlie did not know it, but announcing his last name had lit a recognition inside the man.

They had met before.

When it was clear that Charlie did not realize their shared history, the man finally took his outstretched hand, presenting him with a weak handshake.

"I'm looking for someone," Charlie started.

The man instantly began shaking his head as he attempted to get to his feet.

"No, no," Charlie insisted, "I'm not out to apprehend anyone. I wanted to know if a woman has ever been out here. One who showed up recently."

The man scoffed. "Lots of women out here. More than most suspect, I think."

"This woman is alone, or so the belief is."

"Alone? Out here? Musta misheard your tip." He frowned, as though he found this somewhat unbelievable. Or maybe unconscionable. Charlie got an awful sick feeling. Whatever a woman faced out here, a man would face too. What had this man seen and endured?

He wanted to ask. It would only be right to ask, he told himself. Time to stop towering over him, take up a seat on the cold December ground, talk to him like he would any other person. But when he shifted, his starched collar rubbed at his neck.

Charlie nodded and took a step to the side. As he made his way across the encampment, he glanced behind his shoulder in a way that let Walter know he was leaving him to do a job.

Walter tried to smile at the man at the campfire, but he got the feeling he looked more like a wounded cat.

When he got close enough, he did sit down on the ground, the cold chewing at him through his pants. "I saw her," he whispered. "The one the cop is asking about."

The man's eyes only grew more suspicious.

"She wears a—kind of a cloak. A hood," Walter said, moving his hands over the top of his head.

"Ah!" the man brightened. "You're talking about the angel."

"Angel?" Walter repeated. "You know her?"

"No. She brought me something, though. I don't know how she had it. I left it—with a man. In exchange for help. Some money. I've always needed money, it seems. But he helped me, and I—I lost it. Yet again. I was feeling pretty low, thinking I deserved to be here. But she brought me this. The same thing I left with the man in exchange for the money."

He reached into his coat pocket and pulled out a photograph. A family portrait, old and yellowing. A couple with children. "That's me, when I was a kid," he said, pointing. "'Bout your age. I didn't want to give this up, but I told myself I didn't need it. I knew what my family looked like. Don't know why he let me use it to get money. Just—paper."

"Money's paper, too, I guess," Walter offered.

The man grinned. "Yeah," he said, his teeth flashing out from behind his dark beard. "Guess it is."

"What'd you need money for?" Walter dared to ask.

"Get out of town." The man ran his fingers, pink from the cold, along the edge of the photograph. "I used to be a public servant. Right here. In Sullivan. Bet you didn't know that."

Walter shook his head.

"The town council had budget shortfalls. I was unmarried, no child, and so I was the first to have my hours and pay cut back. Couldn't pay rent. I was getting kicked out of my home. So much for footloose and fancy-free, huh?"

"But you got money."

"Yeah, I got money. And then I got robbed." The man shook his head.

"You should have asked again."

"For what—more of what I already lost?"

"You said you were robbed."

"Well, then, didn't keep safe."

Walter shifted, uncomfortable; his shoes pinched at him, offering a reminder of how hard it could be to ask for something you needed.

"I could never get myself together after that. Years, it's been going on. Two steps forward, fifty back. One tragedy after another. One town after another. Till I wound up back here. It's so easy to lose your way and so hard to get back on track. You don't know about that." Quietly, he added, "Hope you never do, son."

Walter offered a half-grin. "But you got your picture."

"I did at that. And the man she was with gave me some boots!" he added, pointing at his feet. "Said he'd only worn them a few times. Said I needed them more than he did."

"Shoes are important." Walter jumped at the chance to say it.

"So strange how I got these things," the man told him. "Out of nowhere—like some kind of miracle. On Thanksgiving night, when I didn't have anything. And she said, I'll never forget—'There's strength in you still.'"

The man's eyes watered. "Can you believe it?"

He gazed off behind Walter's shoulder, in the direction of the not-so-distant depot. He slid his photograph back in his pocket. "I'm going home. Next train that can take me there. Got a brother in Kansas. I always thought they wouldn't want to see me, some broken down old thing. But—"

"'There's strength in you still,'" Walter recited.

"Yeah. Maybe there is. Without her coming by, though—maybe I never woulda seen it."

"Now you really are getting back on track," Walter said, nodding at the rails behind him.

They smiled at each other, and Walter felt a warmth of pride about his cleverness.

"You find her, you tell her Frank is on his way home. You tell her—you tell her he loves her. Whoever she is."

Walter promised. "Thanks for talking to me," he said, standing.

"Why you looking for her, anyway?"

"She might…need help herself," Walter said, borrowing Charlie's half-lie.

"I don't think you're gonna find her. Angels are like whispers.

You can't catch 'em up in your hands."

"Good luck. With everything," Walter told him, holding out his hand for the man to shake—the first time in his life he'd ever done it. And only because he'd seen Charlie do it a moment ago.

"Thanks. And if you find that woman, you thank her for me, too. I mean it. Not just for the shoes. Thank her for…" The man thought a minute, his eyes glittering again. "Sometimes, you have to *remember*. Or—maybe it's that your memories kinda get fogged up, and you need somebody to clean 'em so you can see right again. See the truth in them."

He looked behind Walter, toward Charlie. He was glad that Charlie did not suspect that his last name was Talbot. That he had once been a police officer in Sullivan. And he had once caught a ten-year-old boy in the midst of stealing a cast iron toy.

Funny how tragedy could be a disguise like no other. Perhaps because we could never bear to find someone who had been close to us living beneath tragedy's mask. Frank knew well that if it was too hard to see, people simply…didn't.

As for Walter, he was almost giddy. He was right about the strange woman. He *knew* he was—but now, here, proof of her kindness.

"Come on," Charlie insisted, grabbing Walter roughly by the shoulder. "We have to go."

"Go where?"

"Get in the car. We have to catch up to her."

"Who?" Walter asked.

Charlie threw open the door of his patrol car and he motioned for Walter to hurry up.

"Who?" Walter asked again, settling into the front seat.

"The woman. In the cloak. I saw her over there in the woods,"

Charlie said, and slammed the passenger door shut.

114

16.

HETTY TRUDGED ALONG. MERELY walking such a long distance would have been bad enough, but here she was having to tug each step from heavy snow, and it was utterly exhausting her. The cane she brought along wasn't helping much. Fatigue saturated her deepest marrow. Why did it have to snow again late last night? Why was the world determined to throw every frozen obstacle in her way? Why did she get this idea of hers so late? Here it was nearly December, with so much to do. Time was a wolf tracking her scent.

She needed her work to be done well before Christmas Eve. Hetty knew the people of Sullivan. She knew that the surprise miracle of a family trinket would make them want to turn around and extend a little miracle of their own. It would not matter to them that they had no way of returning a favor to Hetty—primarily because they did not know she was the one orchestrating the returns. They would simply want to extend that feeling to anyone—and they would. Christmas would be different that year because of it. It would shine with a thousand little kindnesses, glitter with simple unexpected gestures.

But Christmas would only be different if Hetty returned the trinkets with plenty of time left for the people of Sullivan to come up with their own glad tidings, to be left on one another's doorsteps.

She told herself not to worry. She would get through this, as she'd gotten through everything else. Snow and old bones were no matter when you were Bonwit tough.

Up ahead—so very far, it seemed to her—there it was, the edge of the woods. She could already make out the red brick of the Pendleton home, the smoke curling up from the chimney. The end was in sight. One thing she could find gratification in was that not many people in Sullivan knew their town as well, or would have been able to make it through the woods on their own like this. No one else would have been able to use the woods as she was, relying on them to keep her hidden during daylight hours.

Each step she took gave her a sense of pride. *Still got it, old girl,* she teased herself.

She maneuvered past the clearing and started to drag herself to the kitchen door, where she knew she would find Ida. She had barely left the trees behind when a wave of weakness like nothing she had ever felt hit her. It was only a few feet, but it now might as well have been a hundred miles.

She swayed.

She did not think she could lift one foot. Not one more time.

This couldn't be happening to her. Not now. Not when she was this close.

Hetty had come for a couple of reasons—to give Ida the old item of Frankie's, but also to see if the Pendletons could spare any food. Not for her, but for the Rossi family.

Last night, as she and Bernard had gone about their after-dark trinket returns, she had seen the cat carved into the Rossi fence. "Reminds me of Gent," Bernard had said of Mrs. Rossi's habit of feeding any of the men from the Hooverville who happened to knock at her back door. Hetty had wanted to leave something with her right then—she had wanted Bernard to help her think of something she could do for the Rossi woman—but their Tin Lizzie had begun to cough and sputter, threatening to conk out completely, right there in front of the Rossi house. Everyone would have wanted to know what she and Bernard were doing out there in the dead of night.

She could not risk it. This whole plan of hers hinged on not being recognized. And so they had headed back home.

No Rossi had ever come to the Bonwit house, asking for help. There was nothing to return to the Rossis. But Hetty wanted desperately to do something for them. Help in some way. Now that Gent was gone and Hetty was herself winding down, she took comfort in the fact that Mrs. Rossi was still in town.

Her desire to help was powered by her love, still lingering, for her husband. How she missed him, her sweet Gent.

Hetty had decided food would help the Rossis. Any of the Pendleton leftovers. Knowing Ida, all Hetty had to do was plant the idea in her head, and it would not be a one-time occurrence but a regular event. Each night after work, there she'd be, bringing the Rossis any morsel that the Pendletons did not need.

Hetty would not try to hide herself from Ida. Not her true identity. That old cloak of hers would never be enough to conceal her, not from such knowing eyes. There would be a kind of power in showing herself to Ida, in letting her in on her intentions. Hetty was also certain that this secret of hers would not be betrayed.

That was the magic of Ida.

But the *tiredness*…Hetty couldn't talk to Ida without resting first. She needed to sit a moment. Catch her breath.

At her side stood a little wooden building, so rickety these days—the old ice house out behind the Pendleton home.

She placed her hand on the door.

All that remained inside to sit on was an overturned wooden crate that had delivered fruit of some kind to the Pendleton house. Probably for one of their big shindigs. Even in the midst of hard times, the Pendletons still held their parties, often for guests in from out of town.

Hetty tugged her items free from the pocket of her wool skirt. Looking at them gave her a surge of purpose. What funny things to find inspiration in: a list of tasks in her shaky, aging handwriting and a gun that could not even shoot anymore.

Hetty grunted settling onto the crate. The journey had been so hard on her that she could feel her pulse rippling about along the skin on her thighs.

She patted the items in her lap and smiled. Yes, she thought to herself, she could get warm in here. Or, if not warm exactly, at least get out of the winter wind. Take a moment to compose herself.

Just for a little while, she promised herself. Against her will, her eyelids drooped, and she drifted off to sleep.

17.

AT THE SAME TIME Hetty's head was dropping down toward her chest and sleep was overtaking her, Petey was out pacing the neighborhood, wondering where his best bud Walter could have gone off to. His disappearance meant the two of them were now missing out on a perfectly good Saturday afternoon.

Petey'd been stuck in the funeral home all morning, and the last thing he was in the mood for right then was to wander about. The fact that Walter was off somewhere without him was a scrape against his skin.

His father had promised Petey he'd be back quickly, but he hadn't been. The whole time Petey'd been there, sitting at the front desk *just in case*, he'd listened to his mother banging about, running through her daily chores, and he'd found himself jealous of dish washing and floor mopping. If only his job could be so simple. He'd stared at the clock, growing angrier and angrier. *Just in case of what?* he'd wondered. It wasn't like the people who came to their business were going anywhere soon. It wasn't like it was going to be rude to make them wait.

Petey knew the truth, though. Knew the reason why his dad had to take the second job. It wasn't that his business had hit hard times. It was the track. Petey hated racing. He hated gambling. When he was grown, he would never gamble. Gambling was as good as throwing money away. Chasing after empty, hazy dreams of winning like a fool.

He was embarrassed for his dad. Embarrassed that he would believe in something so fake. Like believing puppets were real.

Deep down, underneath the anger and embarrassment, Petey was afraid. What was Petey supposed to even do if that door opened? How was he supposed to handle someone bursting through their door in tears? People did that. He'd seen it before. How was he supposed to pat their hand or put an arm around their shoulder, like his dad? No one wanted him to do that. Not some ten-year-old kid.

It wasn't the dead that bothered him. That was what bothered all the other boys. Petey was bothered by the living who came, the handkerchiefs saturated with grief and the weight of the worst thing that had ever happened to them. Petey had never lost anyone. All his grandparents were alive. He had never been to a funeral for anyone he had ever loved.

And he did not know what to do or say when a person arrived carrying some suit *for the deceased*, ready to choose a casket.

He was terrified of adding to their awful weight by doing the wrong thing. Not handling their loved one in the right way. Because Petey's biggest secret, the one that he tried to hide from all the other boys with the swearing and the smoking and his hardened ways, was that he was as soft deep down as Walter. Another, as Mrs. Drummond would say, *tenderheart.*

Maybe even more so.

No matter what he did—how many noses he bloodied in neighborhood fistfights or chances he took standing atop Sullivan's highest hill after tightening the leather straps of his roller skates—he could not get tougher. He couldn't understand it. Hands got calluses from being used roughly. Why couldn't he grow calluses, deep down, where it counted?

He'd sweated and he'd watched the clock, and when it was a full hour past the time his father had promised to be back by, Petey finally took their phone off the hook. He couldn't take it anymore. It wasn't a great solution, but it would buy him some time, anyway. If someone couldn't call.

He'd hoped no one would get annoyed with the busy signal and come straight to the funeral home, anger stacked on top of their grief.

When his dad finally showed, Petey'd bolted.

He wanted to be around Walter, who never judged him or cared about things like where his house was or that there were dead bodies downstairs. Walter wouldn't wonder out loud about where his dad had been that morning, either. He would already know about the janitor job and the money lost at the track—he wouldn't have to ask—but he wouldn't care.

Petey hated that he needed that kind of friendly comfort. It made him feel softer than ever.

But he didn't change course. He wandered about the neighborhood, his too-big coat flopping against his body and his breath coming out in big puffy clouds. He wondered where Walter could have possibly gone. He wasn't home, but his mother was—and Petey would rather eat glass than talk to Walter's mother.

The more he looked, the more his anger—ignited by his father and still within reach and easy to find again—began to heat up once more. This time, the burn was directed at his friend. Why wouldn't Walter have waited for him? After Petey had given him the plan about how to get new shoes? Where was he?

Petey paused to fish his cigarettes from his coat. He would find Walter. One way or the other. Even if it took the rest of what was left of his Saturday.

18.

BACK INSIDE THE ICE house, Hetty cracked her eyes open. She wasn't sure how long she'd slept. It felt like a blink. It certainly hadn't been long enough—somehow, the sleeping had further depleted her. She felt even more run-down than she had when she'd stepped inside. She didn't know if she had the energy to get home. She didn't recuperate like she did when she was younger. She couldn't get her breath back.

Would she make it to her evening plans? At that point, she could not quite fathom so much as climbing in and out of a car.

Bernard would insist she take the night off. Thirty years ago, it wouldn't have seemed like much to lose: a night's plans. But now, here, it was enormous. Like losing a decade. Because she didn't have many evenings left. At this point, one night felt tragic.

She was also beginning to realize how hazy the end of her plan still looked. The whole thing would depend on having the right person around after she died. But who? Bernard was slowing down—

maybe not as fast as she was, but…

This was all beginning to feel dangerously precarious.

Voices began to filter through the wooden door of the ice house. Maybe it was Ida. Maybe Ida could give her some coffee, something to eat. Anything would help her get back home.

Hetty hoisted herself to her feet with her cane. When she finally stuck her head out of the door, she saw a police officer and a little boy coming toward the ice house.

The officer bellowed, "There you are! You! Stop! Stop there!"

With every last shred of strength she could muster, she began to run. Actually run, like she hadn't in half a lifetime. Or maybe that was gallop, like the horses she had ridden as a girl.

But the officer was running, too. And his body was fifty years younger than her own. He was not a rusty hinge, and he easily closed the gap.

It terrified her, maybe being caught. Maybe being found out.

She pushed her pain aside, heading closer to the thick line of trees.

All she could do was hope that this officer didn't know the woods like she did. Hope that he and the boy would be confused by the surroundings, the blinding sameness of snow. She was aware she was losing ground. But she was also aware she could find her way out of any maze, any puzzle.

If only she could keep them at a distance long enough.

If only she could win herself enough time.

THE LAST THING WALTER wanted to do was run on the broken-open blisters inside his awful shoes. The cold bleeding through the leather stung. The open sores burned. And there was something about having already fought the pain for such a long period. He was so tired of having to put up the front of not being bothered by it, when in reality, his jaw ached from clenching his teeth against the pain.

But he couldn't let Charlie reach the woman first.

"I can get her," Walter assured Charlie.

Charlie didn't stop running. But he was weighed down by his belt and his cuffs. He was young, but not a boy anymore. Cold was seeping in; the two of them had been searching the fringes of the woods far longer than he had anticipated. It had not mattered to Charlie that the woman had not been immediately visible. He knew he had seen her—she had to be out there somewhere. How hard could it be, he thought, to see a black spot on a pure white background? But the cold had gotten to him, chewing away at his bare hands and the officer's hat that left his ears exposed. With a wrench in his heart, he had to acknowledge that a wounded child could still be faster than a shivering man approaching middle age.

Walter pressed forward, determined to show Charlie he needn't worry about it—he could leave it up to him. Walter would have torn his feet off in order to get to the woman first.

He had to see her on his own. Look into her face. Was he right about her? Or was he being a fool? Why was she giving back things all over town, like the Westbrook woman said? How was it that she had them in the first place? Was she a thief who was suddenly struck by her conscience?

Now, within reach, here she was. That black cloak. This was his shot to look at her, just the two of them. Eye to eye. Like before.

Would he see something different? Maybe his mother had been right about him all along. Maybe his dumb, silly heart really could lead him astray.

He burned inside—from the cold in his lungs and from being torn apart by so many competing thoughts.

At the edge of the woods, Walter found himself within arm's reach of her. Close enough to grab her—though he would never do such a thing. Not to an adult. Even though she was old, and easily overtaken.

She cowered, leaning on her cane. She tugged her cloak farther across her head, turning her face away from Walter's.

"People in town think you're up to no good," he blurted.

"Why?" she asked, turning her face a little closer. Through the gap in her cloak, Walter thought he saw the fear in her eyes vanish, replaced by a look not unlike the one she had flashed at him through the Drummond window. He could only describe it as a look of kindness.

He melted a bit, despite his resolve to be objective.

"Herman reported a break-in," Walter told her. "At his old restaurant. The police think it's probably you."

"It wasn't to steal," she insisted.

Walter's stomach hurt. "So you were the one in there?"

"It was the opposite of stealing. Please believe me," she begged.

Charlie's footsteps and the jingling of his belt—full of keys and locks and cuffs—grew louder.

Did Walter believe her? Did he trust Charlie? Did she need help?

"Why were you at my house? The other night?" he asked. "You were trying to give us something, weren't you?"

"It's there. I left it. If you'll look. You need to find it before the holidays. For your mother."

Walter ached to know what, but he didn't have time. Not if he wanted to help her get away. "Go," he hissed. When she didn't move right away, he frowned at her. "*Hurry.*"

She disappeared then, her dark cloak somehow getting swallowed up by the white-coated trees.

"What happened?" Charlie wanted to know between pants.

Walter was already asking himself the same thing. Charlie was looking right at him, but not in a harsh manner, with eyes like the light of the interrogation rooms Walter'd seen in Saturday movies with Petey. And he didn't look at him like an adult looked at a child. Not like something that needed to be steered. Not like an obstacle to what he wanted to accomplish. He looked at Walter the way adults looked at each other when they were meeting up, speaking at the same eye-level. As though he was someone who understood the world in the same terms Charlie did. Someone who would know exactly the kind of information Charlie needed.

Walter had never been looked at that way before. Not by an adult.

He should tell Charlie. Tell him that the woman had something to do with Herman's restaurant. She was the one who had broken in. She had admitted as much.

But his eyes landed on Charlie's badge. And he shrugged. "She got away," Walter said. "Took off in the trees—couldn't find her. Too many tracks in too many directions. Don't think she's as old as she seemed at first. I'm not even sure that was a woman," he lied.

Charlie grunted, staring off into the woods.

Walter felt relief wash through him, warm as the first gulp of hot chocolate.

As soon as it arrived, though, he also wondered if what he'd done was right.

Before he could question it too much, a woman's voice cut into the cold afternoon air.

20.

"YOU BACK ALREADY, CHARLIE?"

When Charlie turned, he found himself looking at a familiar face—the same face, in fact, that he had stopped to talk to earlier that morning.

"Ida," he sighed, relived. *Finally,* he thought, *now we'll get to the bottom of this.*

"You decide to come back for that skate after all?" Ida asked. Turning toward Walter, she asked, "Bring a young buddy with you?"

"We're tracking down a tip," Charlie told her.

"Oh, *we* are, are we?" Ida asked, playing along. When she realized he was serious, she grumbled, "Is that right."

Charlie's smile faded. He didn't understand her tone. Then again—he must have interpreted it wrong. Ida never got upset with him.

"I think the woman I'm looking for was just here. Maybe you came out because you saw her, too?"

"Only you, Charlie," Ida said, taking hold of both sides of her red cardigan and tugging them across her middle. She'd come out without a coat, her over-shoe galoshes still sitting in a muddy heap by the back door. She'd only meant to come out to grab firewood for old man Pendleton, now too ancient to get it for himself. She'd been truthful when she told Charlie he was the only one she'd seen. But the mention of seeing a woman made Ida's eyes dart up toward the woods. She thought of Bernard, and she wondered if it had really been Hetty.

"I thought she might need some help—"

"Now, Charlie," Ida interrupted. "You and I have known each other though lots of times. Different times. Good and bad, and through it all, we've been pretty true to one another. I'm going to be real disappointed in you if you start lying to me now."

"I'm not—"

"*Charlie.*" She narrowed her eyes at him.

And there it began—an invisible sort of tug-of-war. Ida was not going to say anything that Bernard wouldn't admit to if he were standing there. Not sweet Bernard, who had helped her walk through the snow to the Pendletons' kitchen door. Bernard, who would be out at the property the next morning, shoveling, just as he promised. Bernard, who was helping Hetty Bonwit, returning all those little items that Gent had saved. It was a good thing Hetty was trying to do. After screaming and running so many Sullivan children off her property. Hetty, it seemed, had seen the error of her ways.

Certainly, Ida thought, such a revelation would not have happened without Bernard, whom Ida considered her own dear friend.

No—Ida would not betray Bernard. Especially not about this.

Ida stared Charlie down, determined that he would see the error of his own ways. The error he had been making with all the

Sullivanites, ever since that Christmas Eve raid at Frankie's speakeasy.

"Now, Charlie, lots of folks around here are needing help these days," Ida said, in a saccharine singsong tone. Obviously fake. "I can't for the life of me figure out *which* person in need you might mean."

At which point, a white explosion rocked against the red shoulder of her cardigan.

Charlie flinched, shooting his hands out to the side, in front of Walter. As though his arms could have ever protected him from the sudden attack.

Only, what *was* the onslaught? Charlie frowned at Ida's shoulder, covered in a scattering of white, still trying to make sense of it when another explosion hit. Followed by giggles.

Snow. Ida was being pelted with snowballs, one after another. Charlie turned his gaze upward, finding the face of a young girl in the window upstairs, her hands scooping snow off the sill.

That time, the girl missed—and hit Charlie instead, the cold smack stinging the side of his face.

A shocked silence pulsed for a moment. Charlie pushed the remaining snow off his cheek.

"See, there, Charlie? Looks like you could use a little help yourself," Ida said.

At which point, a snort and relieved laughter floated down from the upstairs window.

Walter chuckled too. Until Charlie tossed a glare his way.

"I'm trying to find out about a woman on her own," Charlie explained.

"Are you, now. You sure are interested in getting to the bottom of everything these days. You sure are acting all official."

"Official?" Charlie repeated. "I am, in fact, an *officer*. So, yes. I suppose I am."

Why wouldn't he? Why wouldn't Ida want him to be? The people of Sullivan had given him the patrol car and the shortwave to reward him for his good work.

"I can remember a time, not so long ago, when you weren't," Ida said. She was only adding to his anger. They both knew that.

"We grow up. We leave behind our youthful ways," Charlie said.

"That's not it at all," Ida told him.

They stared each other down.

"Ida," he said, "if something is going on in this town, something you know about, you need to tell me. I won't let what happened before happen again. That's why I'm doing this."

Another snowball shot out of the window. Followed by giggles.

Ida didn't budge.

"I'm going to need to look in the Pendleton ice house."

"What for?"

"I'm looking for the woman, I said."

Ida took a breath, squinting at Charlie. She had the town's secret snared there in her teeth. Charlie knew it.

"We," Ida corrected. "You said *we* earlier. The two of you are both looking for this person?"

"Right," Charlie said. Now, this determination of his to be seen as the most official person in town seemed a little ridiculous, considering who his partner for the day happened to be.

"What you got in this, son? Why are you helping Charlie track down some tip?" Ida asked, still searching for a way to keep Charlie away from that ice house. She had no idea why Charlie wanted to look inside. Whether Hetty might herself be in there. If she was, Ida had to protect her.

It was all resting on Ida's shoulders now. She could feel it, like snow heavy enough to bow the roof of a building.

"Me?" Walter said, pointing at his chest. "I'm—I'm—the—deputy…for the—day."

At which point, Ida laughed, relieved. "Now, *that*, I like," she told Charlie.

"I saw someone leave that ice house," Charlie said. "She ran into the woods."

At his side, Walter let out a squeak of protest. When Charlie glanced down, Walter said, "I didn't think—it was even—a woman."

But Charlie wasn't listening. He wasn't interested in Walter. Not right then. It was Ida.

The truth pulsed. It was there, Charlie thought, within reach.

"Hey, kid?" Ida called.

Walter was too afraid to so much as gulp. Had Ida seen him let the woman get away? Was she about to tell Charlie what he'd really done? Would Walter now be in trouble with the Sullivan police? Wind up getting cuffed? Hauled in? There was some law against helping criminals, wasn't there? The strange woman still could be one. Walter had no real proof that she wasn't. Only her words and his gut feeling.

Talk about being late for dinner. His mother was going to be furious.

Ida smiled at him, sensing his fear. "Give the ice house a quick look for the good officer."

Charlie frowned, confused.

Walter stood immobile.

"Go, on, kid. You go give that ice house a look. Tell our friend here if there's anything out of sorts about it."

Walter looked up at Charlie.

"This is an official matter," Charlie started.

"Well, if it's official, that means you need a warrant," Ida reminded him.

When Charlie's eyes swelled, Ida explained, "I learned a few things too after the night of that old raid."

She let that settle in before continuing, "If this is—less official—if it's more about the good people of Sullivan looking out for one another, then your *unofficial* deputy here can give it a look."

A snowball crashed against the side of her head. "Go on. We'll wait," she added, shaking the snow from her hair.

The winter cardinals sang. The woman in the woods got still farther away.

Charlie nodded once at Walter, who trudged up toward the ice house. As he walked, he wondered if the two grown-ups could see his heart thrashing about inside him.

He cracked the door, which squealed against the cold. He found empty shelves. A few footsteps in the earth, dotted by impressions of the round end of a cane.

He found, too, the items that had dropped from Hetty's lap upon standing: a piece of paper and a tiny little gun, so small, it looked fake. And completely useless, as the hammer was missing. Anyone who had ever picked up a copy of *Detective Comics* knew that much. Walter examined the paper, finding a list written on it in handwriting that looked like his grandmother's. A list of names. Walter's mother was on it. With an item beside it. So the woman had been telling him the truth. Walter smiled. His heart hadn't led him astray. He'd been right about her all along.

Walter left the items behind—they were not his, after all—and pulled his head out. At that moment, he felt something hot inside of him. It was defiance, far stronger than anything he might have felt earlier that day, on the bus. Defiance against his mother. Defiance against everyone who had ever told him it was wrong to have such tender feelings. Defiance against the very idea that his heart was troublesome.

He shut the door and he walked back to Charlie's side.

"Well?" Ida asked.

Walter looked right into Charlie's hopeful, searching eyes. "Nothing out of place," he said. "Nothing at all inside. Except for that old fruit crate. Guess you guys haven't gotten your ice delivery yet today."

Another snowball landed against Ida's back. "Glad we got that settled," she said. "And, no—we only get ice deliveries when we're gearing up for a big party. So there wouldn't be anything inside. Thanks, kid." She removed her glasses, the ones she wore at the tip of her nose while cooking, in order to read her handwritten recipes. As she knocked the snow from the right lens, Walter could have sworn he saw her wink at him.

"And now, if you don't mind," Ida said, "I have a little girl I need to tend to, before I can get back to work."

She leaned down, scooped a wad of snow into her bare hands. "Betty Pendleton and I have been playing this game here since she was a little thing. Even though she's a bit too old for this silliness—'bout as old as this deputy here, I suspect—I would never disappoint her by not playing along."

Ida packed the snow tighter as the giggles carried on through the upstairs window. With one last look at Walter, she said, "Some things you should never outgrow."

HOW LONG HAD IT been when Hetty Bonwit emerged from the woods again? Even Hetty wasn't sure. Her body told her it had been weeks, but of course that was a lie. Forty minutes, maybe?

She dragged herself out of the clearing and closer to the Rossis' back door. She wondered if this particular errand was, in fact, a little pointless. What was the phrase? *Fool's errand.* Maybe that was all this was. But for Hetty Bonwit, it was still one she had to complete.

She wished the police hadn't chased her away. She wished she'd had a chance to talk to Ida. She wished she could have gotten food for Mrs. Rossi. The alternative to the food, this other thing she had brought with her just in case her visit with Ida didn't pan out…it was awfully silly. Maybe not worth giving at all.

Of course, she reminded herself, none of the trinkets she was returning were worth anything…the difference here was that this thing had never belonged to the Rossis. And that made it feel like an empty gesture.

She didn't *have* to make her stop at the Rossis' house. But if not then, when? She was so very tired. Not only tired but feeble. She did not know how many of these trips she had left in her. And now, to make her situation even worse, Officer Barister was on her tail.

She swayed a bit on her feet. She never got this weak when she was younger. She never had to fight for air. Her body did not recuperate as it once did. And when it wore down, anymore, down in energy and stamina, she got so, so low. Everything she needed was too far, too high. Everything was out of reach.

She was filled with a sensation of time being so short that each tick of the second hand shrank visibly what time was left. Days were wool in hot water. It made her feel short of breath. Chased. The fire of need burned hot—the desire to act. Now. Do it. There might not be another chance.

And yet—

All she had for the Rossi woman was a silly ring in the pocket of her cloak. A piece of her own costume jewelry. Large and gaudy. She rarely wore jewelry at all anymore. Her arthritic hands made it especially hard to wear rings. Impossible, most times. She had even abandoned her wedding ring, the one piece she had sworn, decades ago, to never take off. The idea had seemed so good when it was new—but anything new always shines a little more.

She had to hurry. If she was going to complete this, her mission, a stranger scattering glittering breadcrumbs.

Oh, but why, oh, *why* couldn't the Rossis have left something with Gent? Why had their name been nowhere on Gent's trinket list?

Her head swam, going back over the same thoughts until they were polished stone. She was dizzy from weakness. So tired from all the running about. So, so tired. She needed something to eat. She was so sick of having to fight her own body.

She turned the ring over in her hand, taking one last look. Maybe, she thought, that last look would push her in the right direction. Even worthless, she told herself, it really was still pretty, wasn't it?

You know what I think the prettiest thing in this whole world is? Hetty asked herself. And immediately answered, *A nice story.*

She had stories. Lots of them. So many. Here, at the end, with nothing of value in her drawers, she still had that. So what if the ring was worthless? It was a piece of yesterday, like the other trinkets. And Hetty could make up a story to go along with it. Wasn't that what made eyes well up when the trinkets were returned? The stories that went along with them?

And—this was the best part—it would be the one give that was purely her own. Even Bernard had offered Talbot his old boots at the Hooverville. This time, though, it would be her idea alone. She would be following Gent's lead. If she couldn't leave Mrs. Rossi money, she would leave her hope. Like Gent had taught her.

That was the best kind of Christmas gift, wasn't it? The feeling of hope and goodness and excitement for what was to come in the new year? Wasn't that what Christmas was always supposed to present us?

Or was that some empty little phrase, something pretty sounding with nothing underneath? Was she simply repeating a familiar refrain, like the melody line of a sweet song?

No matter. She had no time to keep ruminating on any of this. And she did not have time to back out. This was what she had—a worthless ring and a story. She knocked on the door.

And she swayed. She was so dizzy. She was so tired.

She needed food. She'd never get home without some food.

She couldn't ask Mrs. Rossi, though, could she? Take the woman's food, when she had already given so much to the men who lived in the camp behind the depot? That was the opposite of what she had come here to do.

She grabbed for the doorknob. She needed to sit. Get someplace warm. This had been too much.

She had to eat. Just a bite. Rest.

She knocked again. Harder. Had Mrs. Rossi heard her?

She had to get inside. Get warm. Get fed. Give Mrs. Rossi the ring. Before time ran out.

She raised her hand to knock again.

The door swung open.

A little girl stood there to greet her.

22.

PETEY WAS GETTING ANGRIER the longer he walked the streets of his neighborhood. He wondered if Walter was at the library. It was a dumb place to be on a Saturday, but Walter liked it. He liked books and stories.

Petey would go *get* Walter, then. And when he found him, his back curled over some musty old book at his favorite table in the back of the library, Petey would ask him what the big idea was. *What's the big idea, Walt?* just like that. And it would embarrass Walter and even get a few nasty stares and *shhhhh*es from some of the librarians. But Petey had been dumped on twice now—twice!—first his dad leaving him alone and now Walter leaving him alone. And here it was a Saturday. It was wrong to dump on a boy on Saturday.

Petey wouldn't go whining and bawling about it, though. He'd let out his frustration by being rough with Walter.

Petey passed by the retaining wall and headed straight for the easement alongside Hetty's property. It had been traveled plenty that morning, with not so much as a skiff of snow left. The path was a giant stretch of mud, punched with footsteps.

He knew that he was in the right to go this way, and he knew that everyone in town had already *been* this way, but he ducked down just the same. Practically folded himself in half, his chest right there on his knees. That way, he would not be taller than the windows. He would slip on by. No delay brought on by some grumpy old lady. And then he'd be on his way, straight to the library. Off to give Walt a bit of what-for.

Walter would spend the rest of the day making up to him. That's just how he was. Petey knew that. Petey was in the mood at that point to be made up to.

One thing was for sure—Petey was no fool. Not like his dad, throwing all their money away at the track. And not like Walter. He was grateful for Walter, but Walt couldn't even figure out how to ask for shoes. Petey wasn't going to be that way. Not him. Not a chance.

Not even halfway down the path, the front door slapped open at the Bonwit house and out flew Hetty.

At least, Petey assumed it was Hetty.

That day, she seemed especially ferocious, ambling out toward him with an afghan draped over her head and shoulders. She'd come out too quickly to put on her coat this time. Her voice was little more than a high-pitched snarl, and she was on top of him before he had a chance to get out of her way. Swinging her broom like she had been saving up all her energy just for him. Swinging like he was a carnival game, some object meant to be broken open with a hammer to reveal the prize inside.

Petey didn't know it, but that was not Hetty Bonwit at all. Hetty Bonwit was at the Rossi home. This person—so vicious, swinging at him with that broom—was Bernard. Because Bernard thought the best way to help keep Hetty's secret, the one about delivering remembrance trinkets to their rightful owners, was to pretend to be her, at home, right where she should have been.

Even though Bernard was angry at her—angry for breaking her promise to him to stay put, angry for making him worry—he would do anything to protect her wishes. Because even in his anger, he adored her. In his mind, he still saw the woman with the bright green eyes, so happy to introduce him that first day to the Bonwit carriage house. A home away from home. And then, simply—home.

Yes, this way, he thought, if he pretended to be Hetty, it would offer some protection against a Sullivanite recognizing her as she traipsed about the fringes of town that day. *Why, it couldn't have been that old Hetty Bonwit you saw! She was at home, yelling and chasing after my own son!*

No, Petey did not know that it was Bernard. Did not see the difference between the height of the form beneath the afghan and the height of the woman who usually came out after him and Walter. Especially Walter.

Petey assumed it was the same old junkyard-dog Hetty Bonwit. And here she was, coming after him like she'd come after Walter the day before Thanksgiving. Screeching. Sure that he was a soft target.

That was it—that was all Petey could take. Because as she raced toward him, he had to look at himself, at where he was. Cowering. Crouching down, trying not to be seen. Attempting to slink away. Racing to find the friend who was off having a fantastic Saturday without him.

He *was* a fool. No better than his dad. And every bit as soft as Walt. Worse, even—timid and spineless. Petey let out his own wail, even louder than the old woman's. Picking out the perfect target for revenge, he sidestepped Hetty, ran up her front lawn, and kicked her mailbox right off the edge of her porch. The one the neighborhood mailman had placed up there to accommodate her inability to walk well.

Sure. Poor Hetty Bonwit, too old and arthritic to walk. That's what everyone said, when they wanted to offer her some pity. Petey knew better. She could sure come after the neighborhood kids when she wanted.

"What do you even have a mailbox for, anyway, you mean old bat?" Petey cried out. He wanted to be tough. He wanted to show her that he was no sucker. But tears were streaming now. To keep her from noticing the mortifying waterworks, he went on, "Nobody wants to send you anything, anyway."

Bernard remained underneath that afghan, crouched over in Hetty's arthritic way, the blanket draped over his head and hiding his face entirely. He shook his balled fist, snarling at Petey with unintelligible high-pitched words.

For good measure, Petey swung his leg backward. And he put everything he had in one more last good kick, sending the Bonwit mailbox skittering out to the curb.

CHARLIE PULLED THE PATROL car up to a stop at the Drummonds' house. Before he could get the engine turned off, Mrs. Drummond's knuckles began to rap against the driver side window.

Charlie jumped, turned the crank to eliminate the glass between himself and Walter's mother.

"And?" Mrs. Drummond wanted to know.

"Walter was instrumental in the search," Charlie said.

"You found her, then?"

"We have a lead the department can now pursue. Which we would not have gotten without Walter," Charlie informed her, in a voice to match his starched collar.

This relaxed her face a bit. Walter was an extension of herself. If Walter was the reason the woman would be found, then *she* was the reason the woman would be found.

She nodded, as though she had always known this would be the case. "Would you like to stay for dinner, officer?" It was a perfunctory rather than friendly invitation.

"No, ma'am, I need to get back to my own family. Thank you, though."

Mrs. Drummond nodded, flashing the tiniest hint of a relieved smile.

"You can help me with dinner, Walter," Mrs. Drummond said, even though Walter never helped with dinner. This was only Mrs. Drummond's attempt to get Walter close, to drill him for more information.

Charlie rolled up his window. He expected Walter to immediately jump out, put this day behind him. But he sat there staring at Charlie.

"You didn't tell her about the shoes," Walter said.

"I told you I wouldn't."

Yes, that was exactly what Officer Barister had said, outside the shoe store. When Walter had hesitated on the sidewalk beside the entrance, Charlie had put a hand on his shoulder and assured him, *We'll find a pair as close as we can to the ones you already have. No one will notice.* So he'd saved Walter from another day hobbling about in his painful Boy Scout lace-ups, and he'd saved him from having to upset his mother.

Walter kind of felt like cheering all over again, exactly like he had when he'd tossed his old pair in the closest trash bin behind the shoe store.

Charlie nudged Walter. "Scuff the toes up a little on the way in," he said. "Just for good measure."

Walter reached for the handle. But stopped. "*Why* didn't you tell her?"

"I didn't want to embarrass her."

"You can't embarrass her."

"You can embarrass anyone," Charlie insisted. "I didn't want to do that to her. It'll be between you and me."

Walter grinned at Charlie for the first time that day.

But then it came back to him—the fact that he had spilled everything about the strange woman. In the car, as Charlie zipped his Chevy about, trying to catch a glimpse of her—a stark black dot against a sea of white trees. He had told him, trying to convince him to leave her alone. "She's giving people things," he'd begged. But Charlie had seen her again, leading to that chase behind the Pendleton house. Walter had maybe helped the woman get away, but he had also been the reason the woman had nearly been caught.

He'd been rewarded for his information with new shoes. And now, Charlie knew more than Walter wanted him to.

Charlie pointed. "Head on in, now. Your mom said she needs you."

Walter finally consented. He didn't want to. But what else was there to do?

Charlie would have watched to make sure Walter got all the way inside his home, but Walter turned, halfway up his yard, and waved at him as though all was well. No intention of going inside too soon, despite what his mother had asked. So Charlie waved again and he backed down the small gravel drive, back into the street.

Charlie still had a few hours left in his shift. It would be time, then, to head back to the precinct. Exchange the patrol car for the Barister family car. Usually, upon returning home, Charlie would immediately change clothes, change roles. Not that night, though. Charlie knew there would still be a late-night trip. There had to be. Someone needed to check in on Herman's alley door that night. Someone needed to be there in case that woman showed up again. And he figured she would—it was too cold to spend the night traipsing about the woods. Besides, this was his case.

He started to turn the corner; tightening his grip on the steering wheel pinched into that cut on his palm. He grimaced, stopped, turned his hand over to check it, see if it had gotten redder as the day had gone on. Find out if he needed to grab some sort of ointment for it before returning home.

And that was when it happened—it might not have otherwise. If he had not stopped for a moment to look at that silly cut, he might have driven on and missed it completely. But when he raised his head up and looked back out the windshield, he saw it.

Or, really, her. A black blob coming out from the back of the Rossi house. Swaying back and forth as she walked. Moving in and out of the late afternoon haze. And then she was gone.

Charlie sped up, the Chevy growling as he hurried to reach the last spot he'd seen her. How was it that she could disappear so easily? She moved like someone nearly a hundred years old, all that shuffling and swaying back and forth. How could a car not be able to match her speed?

She knew Sullivan. Clearly. But so did Charlie. He circled through the neighborhood, back and forth, up and down streets, snaking down alleyways behind homes.

Nothing. Not a sign of the woman.

As he returned to his original path, he saw Mrs. Rossi coming home, heading up her front walk. Pausing to open her front door. Had the strange woman in the cloak broken in while she was gone?

He pulled to the curb and killed the engine. He gathered up his notebook and he gave the Rossi woman a moment to take her coat off, find out if something was missing. Then, when he showed up, she would be so grateful, she would give him any little piece of information he asked for, no hesitation.

But before he could step from the car, the front door banged open again at the Rossi house.

Out emerged Mrs. Rossi, stomping angrily.

This was it. Surely. She had found something gone.

Charlie pulled himself out from behind the wheel. "Mrs. Rossi?" he called.

She didn't answer. She raced forward.

Her daughter, Elizabeth, chased after her, struggling to keep up.

Charlie broke into a jog. "Mrs. Rossi?"

A bus heading downtown pulled to a stop.

Mrs. Rossi boarded. Elizabeth lunged inside.

Charlie jumped back to the patrol car. Started the engine. And he began to follow the bus.

He followed them all the way downtown.

The bus paused at the curb and the Rossis exited. Charlie tugged the keys from the ignition, all in one swift yank, and hurried around the front fender to see where the Rossis were going.

Mrs. Rossi had not merely been walking before she'd boarded the bus. She'd already been moving too fast for that. But now, she was absolutely flying, her hair rustling backward, away from her face as she pressed forward. Her arms flopping. Harsh footsteps warning any other pedestrians to get out of her way. Elizabeth's own walk, first punctuated by little hops in her struggle to stay close to her mother, turned into an outright sprint.

Mrs. Rossi slowed a bit to grab hold of a store entrance and say something—it looked a little harsh—to her daughter.

The girls disappeared inside.

Charlie gave them a minute to get away from the entrance, then slipped inside the same business, beneath a sign that read *Rosen-*

baum Jewelry and Optician.

149

24.

THE INTERIOR OF THE jewelry store felt hot to Charlie after so much time out in the cold that day—the newsstand, the Hooverville. A sticky kind of sweat instantly formed under his arms, beneath his coat.

But he knew, too, that the sweat wasn't just about the heat.

He started to approach Mrs. Rossi, but he stopped when he saw the way her jaw was set, the way she clenched her teeth. As she stood, she tightened her grip on her pocketbook—not out of fear or concern. Out of anger.

Mrs. Rossi was mad.

Why? Had something really been stolen?

If it had, why the need to go straight to a jeweler?

"Hi, there," Charlie heard—high pitched, coming from his side.

Charlie expected to find someone standing right beside him, trying to get his attention. Instead, he saw Elizabeth Rossi approaching an older woman in the optical section. A Fitzweather, if Charlie remembered right. Something that started with an "M." Martha? Margaret? Church pianist. Loudest belter of "Bringing in the Sheaves."

"Hi," Elizabeth said again.

The Fitzweather woman simply gave her a cool look, then glanced up toward the counter, as if expecting—or at least hoping—that Mrs. Rossi would correct her daughter, get her to come stand beside her.

But Elizabeth persisted. She lifted the woman's glasses—a somewhat fragile wire pair—from the small optician table in front of her and looped them over her ears.

She blinked at the woman, her eyes looking magnified behind the lenses.

The woman chuckled at her in the way she surely chuckled at her grandchildren, relenting at their insistence that they play a game. "Are your eyes bad?" she asked Elizabeth. "Can't you see? Did your mother bring you here for a pair?"

"I don't need glasses," Elizabeth proclaimed. "I can't see anything through yours. That's why I like them. I don't have to see what's coming."

"Oh, shoo, you," the woman said, taking her glasses back.

Elizabeth didn't go back to her mother, though. She lingered in the optical section of the store, sticking her hands deep in the pockets of her coat.

Charlie wandered in her direction, acting as though he was simply ambling about, a cop on his beat, stepping inside to get warm. "What don't you want to see coming?" he asked Elizabeth.

She took a half step back, stuck a finger in her mouth to bite at the nail. And then, as though relieved to be able to say it out loud: "Mom getting mad at me some more."

"More? She's already mad?"

"I gave someone money," Elizabeth said. "She didn't want to take it, but she needed it."

Goosebumps danced down Charlie's arms, even in the heat of the store. "Who?" he asked, his mind filling with the image of the black cloak circling around from the back of the Rossi home. "Who did you give money to?"

"A woman."

"The one you were just talking to?" he asked, playing a bit dumb.

She shook her head. "Someone at my back door."

Charlie wanted to grab the girl and shake her like a penny bank. Let everything she knew spill out of her like saved-up coins.

"Was she—did she have a cloak or a hood on?"

"How did you know?" Elizabeth asked. "Like Little Red Riding Hood. Only black."

Charlie shuddered. Little Red Riding Hood? How did he get to this point—having to get information from children? How could this be? Was she too young to even understand who she was speaking to? Who she saw? What the woman was after? How did you even go about squeezing information out of someone who interpreted the world in storybook terms?

"She took money?" Charlie pressed.

"She wanted something to eat."

"So you fed her?" Charlie asked.

Elizabeth nodded. "Mom was out working. I was alone. Mom always gives food to the men who stop by. Why wouldn't I give some food to her? Some of our dinner? I had it all planned out. I was going to let Mom and Dad eat, and pretend I'd already eaten before they got home. I gave her *my* dinner. Why can't I give what's mine?"

Her eyes got a little shiny and she wiggled her mouth, a dam against tears.

And suddenly, Charlie saw her. He saw Elizabeth. Not a child. A person who had watched her mother extend kindness and wanted to do the same. A person who understood hunger and need. A person that knew she could help, even though she was small. And so she did. She did help that woman.

And now, he was seeing her regret. Born, he knew, from the anger her mother had expressed at her daughter's good deed. A deed not unlike any of her own.

"Something else happened." Charlie spoke as gently as he did when soothing a tear-wracked Tom.

"She gave me a ring. A very fancy ring. To pay for the food. She said—a *king* had owned it."

Charlie's eyes went up to Mrs. Rossi at the counter.

"But I told her it was too much. For just one dinner," Elizabeth insisted.

"So you tried to pay her for it," Charlie guessed, a new wave of astonishment crashing into him. She understood *too much*—understood value. And money.

"I did pay her," Elizabeth agreed. "But she wouldn't take all of it. Just a little. Still. It was the money Mom had been saving. In case of—"

"—the bank going broke," Charlie finished.

"*Yeah,*" Elizabeth whispered, looking up at Charlie with large round eyes still shiny with tears.

"Your mom's here, though. Talking to the jeweler. To find out about the ring, right? Maybe it's worth far more than you gave the woman. You were just trying to be fair. Doing what you thought was right. And most likely, your mom will get money from that jeweler.

And I bet you'll have far more money for Christmas presents than you would have had otherwise."

Elizabeth shook her head. "No," she said, the tears closer than ever now. "No, Mom said the ring is junk. She said I got taken. Said Mr. Rosenbaum would prove her right."

Charlie felt it right along with her—the pain of being turned into a fool.

Until the jeweler burst out from the back, carrying something small in his hands. He beelined for Mrs. Rossi, placed his loupe on the counter. His face was pale, his mouth slack, eyes round.

"Where did you get this?" he asked, loud enough for Charlie to hear.

Mrs. Rossi fidgeted with the top button on her coat. She glanced about the store, until her eyes landed on Elizabeth. She shot her a look of disapproval and waved Elizabeth closer.

After Elizabeth had settled into place at her mother's side, Charlie began to make his own way up to the counter—but not close enough for the group to notice him standing there. He tucked himself over by the wall, near the display window.

"I—inherited it," Mrs. Rossi lied. "Like I told you."

The jeweler shook his head, running a hand through his hair. "I can't pay you for this."

"Why not?" Mrs. Rossi asked, offended. "We got it honestly."

"No—Mrs. Rossi. I believe you. I do. But I can't pay you what it's truly worth."

Now it was Mrs. Rossi's turn to have the color drain from her face. "What *is* it worth?" she asked. She spoke so softly, she leaned forward to make sure Mr. Rosenbaum could hear her.

The jeweler giggled. And then he shrugged. And giggled some more. "I don't know," he admitted. "Surely more than any person—or business—in this town has on hand. More, perhaps, than you'd find in the vault in the Bank of Sullivan. Part of me thinks more than all the gold in Fort Knox."

155

BERNARD TOSSED THE GREASY rag into the bin in the corner of the Bonwit garage. He lowered the door and he glanced up and down the street.

No Hetty.

He started up the front yard, the snow clumping along the sides of his shoes.

He opened the front door. The house felt every bit as empty as one of Gent's gutted music boxes. A loneliness like nothing Bernard had ever felt, not once, not inside the city limits of Sullivan, invaded him. His voice broke as he called out, "I got the plugs replaced." He touched the nape of his neck and cleared his throat, feeling shaky. "Mrs. Bonwit? It should run much smoother now. We can feel free to head out tonight. Again."

The only response he got was the cat, Reginald, a former stray not unlike himself, jumping from the old settee and racing to swirl in and out of his legs, making a figure eight.

So intense was Bernard's worry at that point that it felt like poison in his veins. The muscles in his legs felt pulled.

"I had hoped she would come home while I was working on the car," he told Reginald. "I couldn't drive around looking for her with the car in the shape it was. I had to make sure it wouldn't die on me."

Reginald continued to swirl.

"But I had hoped she'd be back by now," Bernard whispered. Hetty Bonwit had been gone since the morning—or so he had to assume. She had not returned.

And now, it was almost evening.

"I don't know the woods like she does," Bernard admitted. "Hetty learned trees from her father. The lumber business, you know. I could get lost looking for her. Then what good would I be?"

Reginald rubbed his head on Bernard's leg.

What if someone had seen Hetty skulking about a back door? What if someone had misinterpreted what she was doing?

Where was she?

Why did seconds take so long to pass?

Why was the mantle clock so loud?

"Did you hear his anger?" he asked Reginald, thinking of his interaction with Petey earlier that afternoon, the one in which he'd played the role of Hetty. "What if everyone else is equally as angry? Annoyance, I knew about. But anger? Someone could do something truly awful to her. A kicked mailbox is of no matter, but…oh, I'd hoped she'd be back. How do I go about looking? Where do I start? What if she's in those woods? That can't be where she is—can it? But where else?"

Bernard reached down to pet Reginald and saw it, finally—a folded-up note on the floor.

He snatched it up, his heart sinking when he did not find Hetty's flowery handwriting. It was a man's script, thanking her for his own years in the carriage house. For his rescue.

The way he wrote—it brought it all back to Bernard, though it had not really ever been all that far. But there it was, all around him. All those years of tidying up the carriage house and growing flowers for the guests and cooking. Being a part of the Bonwit family—right alongside Gent with his proper ways and Hetty with the green eyes that always looked as though she had just been through a round of belly laughter. They'd let Bernard love them and become part of their world. A contributor to the ongoing good deeds out there in the carriage house. Giving him a purpose, making him belong—that had been a rescue, too. Every single day, he'd been rescued all over again.

Reginald purred, oblivious.

"I will not rest until I fulfill Gent's wishes, Mrs. Bonwit," the letter concluded. And it was signed, "Arthur K. Pulcheck, Esquire."

Bernard would not rest, either.

"I have to go look," Bernard told Reginald, heading for the hall closet to retrieve his coat and hat. "I can only hope Ida has her in the Pendleton kitchen, warming her up with a cup of tea."

Bernard had failed the Bonwits when he had lost their music box all those years ago.

He could not fail them a second time.

26.

CHARLIE WATCHED IRVING ROSENBAUM—still visibly shaken—glance about the interior of his jewelry store. At this point, Charlie was not the only one watching the small group at the counter with interest.

Mr. Rosenbaum cleared his throat and said—a little louder than was necessary, it seemed to Charlie, almost as though he were speaking to the entire room—"See here, Mrs. Rossi?"

He made a motion for her to come closer. She did, leaning her face over Mr. Rosenbaum's hands.

Elizabeth inched forward, placing her fingertips on the counter and trying to stand on her tiptoes, making a kind of grunting noise to tell the adults she would like to see, too.

They ignored her. As adults always ignored children.

Charlie got a pang for the girl—but only a brief one. His attention pinged right back to Mr. Rosenbaum. He inched closer, where he might better hear their conversation.

"See this mark?" Mr. Rosenbaum continued, still in an over-ly loud, stiff voice. "That's why I can tell this is a fake. Nothing but costume jewelry. A nice bit of costume, perhaps, but—nothing but foil-backed rhinestones."

Mrs. Rossi frowned, disappointment crashing across her features. "But I thought you said—"

"That second look will get you every time," Mr. Rosenbaum announced, putting the ring in her hand and leading her toward the door. Elizabeth followed her mother so closely her toes scraped the back of her mother's heel.

Mrs. Rossi let out a little yelp. But when she turned to Elizabeth, she wasn't angry or annoyed. She was drained, having been wrenched from one emotion to another. First fury, then fear at learning what Elizabeth had done with the money. Then hope when Mr. Rosenbaum had tried to indicate her ring was actually valuable. And now, here, the weight of empty pockets and a reality that was only brown and worn-thin. Mrs. Rossi's look told her daughter it would be nice if she would take a step or two back. And it acknowledged, at the same time, that it didn't really matter. What was one more scrape? One more hurt?

Did a person ever get lucky enough to get numb?

"Sorry I couldn't help you this holiday," Mr. Rosenbaum apologized. "But perhaps your aunt has other pieces. Did you happen to inherit—"

"No," Mrs. Rossi moaned. "Just the one."

Mr. Rosenbaum smiled yet another apology and opened his store entrance.

The bell on the door jingled as the two girls were ushered onto the sidewalk.

But Mr. Rosenbaum did not wave and shut the door behind

them.

He went with them.

Charlie felt his heart pick up the pace. This was suspicious. What else did Mr. Rosenbaum possibly have to say to Mrs. Rossi? Wouldn't he simply want to get rid of her, if he had just disappointed her? Wasn't that what everyone did, once they had dealt a setback of some kind?

Charlie walked closer to the plate glass, where more affordable watches had been placed on display. Always the practical objects in the windows those days, not the ones that merely glittered.

Mr. Rosenbaum continued to talk to Mrs. Rossi, even as the snow fell on the tops of their heads and the shoulders of Mr. Rosenbaum's shirt. His face—he was so sincere, so serious. He was talking to Mrs. Rossi slowly, emphasizing certain ideas by gesturing with both hands. Pointing at her ring. He wanted her to take what he was saying to heart. So important was this message that he did not seem to take note of the cold or the snow dancing along the top of his bald head.

What was he telling her? It looked like instructions. Steps he wanted her to follow? But why, if the ring was worthless?

Charlie glanced behind his shoulder. He was the only one with any interest left. Everyone else had gone back to their own reasons for being in the shop, fiddling with their broken watch, or staring at their scratched spectacles. Each of them wondering if their possession could be saved. Wondering what the cost of their little misfortune might be.

It was, after all, the only reason anyone came to a jewelry store anymore. Not to buy new, but to fix what had gone wrong.

Except for Mrs. Rossi. Coming in here with the strange woman's ring.

Was that woman a con artist? To what end? Why trick a little girl? What had she gotten out of it? A meal, certainly, but did she really need it? Walter had told him the woman was leaving items behind. Or returning items. That didn't sound much like someone in danger of starving to death, did it?

And what could be so important for Mr. Rosenbaum to speak this way to Mrs. Rossi?

Mr. Rosenbaum patted Mrs. Rossi on the shoulder.

Mrs. Rossi nodded, still a bit bewildered as she staggered back toward the bus stop. Elizabeth walked along behind her—not as closely this time.

When Elizabeth caught sight of Charlie's face in that window, she smiled. Not a polite smile. Not something she had learned from her mother, a gesture of courtesy. That was a winning smile. A smile from a girl who had just been proven right.

The entrance to the store jingled, and Mr. Rosenbaum walked back in. He smoothed what was left of his hair, smearing the snowflakes across his scalp more than he managed to dust them off. He straightened his shirt and tie. Always a tie to work downtown. It was simply back to his job at the counter, then.

But something had changed in his face. Something had happened, beyond giving a value for a ring.

Charlie approached the glass display case that supported Mr. Rosenbaum's cash register. "Can I ask you about the appraisal you gave the Rossis?" he asked.

Mr. Rosenbaum flinched, surprised and offended. He flashed a face at Charlie that said he did not appreciate the eavesdropping. "Those are confidential," he said.

"Seemed to me you were giving her that appraisal awfully loudly," Charlie said. "Purposefully loud."

Mr. Rosenbaum flashed him another look, this time one of

annoyance.

"Besides, it's part of an investigation."

"What, you think it's stolen?" Mr. Rosenbaum shook his head and busied himself with straightening his counter. He leaned to the side, glancing behind Charlie. He waved at the next person in line—the older woman with the spectacles that Elizabeth had tried on.

"I'm not sure. I certainly don't think Mrs. Rossi stole it herself. I think it was given to her daughter. By a woman in a black cloak."

Mr. Rosenbaum's eyes widened, his face going slack. "Black cloak, you say?"

"You've seen her."

"Think it's an odd detail is all."

"It's more than that. You have seen her."

Mr. Rosenbaum sighed and held up a finger, signaling to the older woman that he would return in a moment. And then he motioned for Charlie to follow him to the back.

PETEY WISHED HIS ANGER hadn't left him so quickly. But it had vanished, all in an instant, when he'd seen that cop car. It had been such a relief to finally see him—Walter, his best bud—that the fire of annoyance had been hit with an entire avalanche of snow.

He'd lingered up at the end of the street, trying to tap back into the hard feelings he'd had for Walter. Leaving him all alone on a Saturday. Of all the rotten things.

Only…Walter hadn't left him, not really. He hadn't just wandered off, or chosen someone else to spend his day with. Not if a police officer was bringing him home. Petey couldn't exactly stay mad at Walter for that.

Besides, curiosity was a powerful thing. It could win out over all other emotions. Curiosity was always the strong man at the carnival.

He raced to Walter's house, his too-big coat flopping against his body with every step.

"What was that all about?" Petey called out. Walter was only halfway up the front yard, but Petey wanted to make sure he stopped him before he had a chance to go inside. Petey pointed down the street, in the general direction the police car had driven. "That thing with the cop? Why'd he bring you home?" He lit a cigarette and offered a crooked grin. "You try to rob Sullivan Bank using your cap gun?"

He was surprised at the way Walter frowned at him.

A voice carrying Walter's name turned the boys' attention toward the street. Herman waved from the rolled-down window of his Plymouth—an unmistakable ride, considering it had absolutely no chrome details and off-colored junkyard fenders. "Walt! You find her?"

"Find who?" Petey wanted to know.

"Officer Barister had him out looking for a woman who broke into my restaurant last night," Herman told Petey.

"*You?*" Petey asked, his grin a tease.

When Walter didn't laugh or offer him a soft punch on his shoulder, Petey tugged his cigarette from him lips. "This has to be a joke. Right?"

"She didn't break in," Walter grumbled.

"Horsefeathers!" Herman said, wiping sweat from his forehead. "She was trying to get into Walt's place here, too."

"No, she wasn't," Walter told Petey, but it did nothing to shrink Pete's wide-open eyes. Shock was keeping him from so much as blinking.

"Yes, she was," Herman insisted. "Your own mother dragged you downtown today to make sure Charlie knew about it."

"She's not a thief," Walter said.

"Then you *did* find her today."

Walter searched for something to tell Herman to make him

back off. He thought of the list he'd seen in the ice house. He tried to remember if Herman's own name was on it. He couldn't be sure.

"Oh, phooey," Herman said, drawing his head back into his car.

He put the Plymouth in gear and started to take off when a Model T honked its Ahooga horn—Bernard warning Herman not to pull in front of him.

Herman squealed to a stop, allowing for the Model T to putter on by.

Once Bernard had gone, Herman shook his head at Walter—one last time—and took off down the street.

"Who's this woman?" Petey pressed. "A regular Bonnie Parker?"

In Walter's face, Petey saw the slightest twinge of regret, as though he didn't want to go on with this story.

"No. Not like that at all," Walter finally said. "She was just trying to make me laugh."

"She broke into your house to make you laugh?" Petey wondered what was wrong with Walter. This story of his wasn't making much sense at all.

"People have her wrong. Besides, she didn't break in. She was looking in my window. That's all. "

"But the cop wanted you to help him with that?" Petey persisted. "Tracking her down? Doing what? Interviews and stuff? Dick Tracy stuff?" Petey was intrigued. The awfulness of his own day receded completely.

"I guess. Yes. Interviews."

"What was it like?" Petey honestly wanted to know.

"We didn't find anything," Walter lied. "We probably never will."

"Still. Riding with a cop all day," Petey said, impressed. Then, "Did you know you were going out with him? Yesterday? When we were at school? Did you know it then? Why didn't you tell me?"

"I didn't know—not all of it—I just..." Walter was too tired to explain. "Mom wants me in."

"You're choosing your *mom* over being out here with me?"

"No, it's just that—she's after me, and I needed to look for something first."

"I can help. You drop something?" But as he started to follow Walter up toward the house, Petey remembered what he'd wanted to tell him, before the cop car and Herman. What he had been thinking of the last hour or so.

"Hey!" Petey said. "Listen, we've got to do something to teach that dumb old Hetty Bonwit a thing or two. She's out of control."

Walter's shoulders drooped. "Not tonight, Petey. I have to do this first."

But what he set about doing was ridiculous—searching in the bushes, the cluster planted right there by the front of the house. Bending branches back and forth, knocking snow out of the way.

"No—tonight," Petey insisted. Even as he said it, though, he felt bad for coming to Walter with this now. He looked pink with cold and his eyes were half-shut and he really did seem exhausted. It was a strange kind of exhausted to see on someone Walter's age. It was more the kind of exhausted Petey saw on his dad, especially when he was dragging himself back home from the track. It was an exhausted that usually had years of disappointment in it. Petey wondered, staring at Walter, how he could have gotten all that in one afternoon.

"You know how it is," Petey said. "She's awful to us. She was awful to you right before Thanksgiving." As he spoke, he felt it inside of him again—the anger, but also the hot poker of revenge jabbing at him.

Walter shook his head, which shocked Petey. Walter never refused Petey outright.

"We've got to strike back to make her stop once and for all," Petey said.

Walter ignored him. Petey didn't think Walter had ever ignored him. Not once in all their weekends and school recesses. He was only tugging at some dumb old bushes by his house. What could Walter possibly care about bushes for? Why wasn't his best bud every bit as important?

"Come on," Petey growled, sticking his cigarette back in his mouth, freeing up his hand to grab onto Walter's sleeve.

But he didn't have to.

Walter stopped all on his own.

There it was, the same item Walter had seen on the list in the ice house. There it was, at his feet, in the snow under the bushes, in the same spot where the woman had stood. In the last glow of afternoon light, there it was—a shiny metal object.

The same object that Hetty Bonwit had feared might not be found in time for the holidays.

CHARLIE'S PULSE WAS A whirlpool in his ears as he stepped into the jeweler's workshop. Inside, an employee was bent over a table, a magnifying lens attached to a band around his head.

"You worked through your afternoon break," Mr. Rosenbaum observed. "Why don't you knock off early?"

The employee raised his head, wearing the look of a person absorbed in a task—a person who would rather work late or skip a meal than leave his momentum behind. But the sight of Officer Barister made him nod once, slip his magnifier off, and tell Mr. Rosenbaum, "See you tomorrow."

Once the door closed, Mr. Rosenbaum folded one arm across his midsection and cupped his mouth with his free hand. The weight of a story filled the room.

Charlie braced himself, feeling a confession might be coming. That Mr. Rosenbaum, to stay afloat, had resorted to other means besides adding optical services at his jewelry store. That perhaps he had been engaged in some sort of scam. If that were true, Charlie knew it would be heartbreaking to take him in. A hard-working man faced with impossible decisions.

"A woman came," he started. "In the black cloak."

"Why didn't you file a report?" Charlie asked.

"Because she didn't steal. Or break in. It was Thanksgiving night. I had come to check on a few things. Hadn't even really planned on being at the shop. She knocked on the back door. At first, I was going to ignore it, but it was so insistent. And it was the holiday—that puts you in a different frame of mind, I suppose. She called out to me."

"She called your name?"

"Yes."

Mr. Rosenbaum was so much older—decades, it seemed—than he'd been the day Charlie and his bride-to-be had come to the shop to pick out their rings. Or maybe, Charlie thought, he and his fiancée had been impossibly young, the two of them like fresh blooms that did not know that love was itself a living thing. One that existed on its own, and so many times, all you were doing was guessing about how to take care of it. More water, more sun, who knew really how much it needed? All the things you were supposed to do, but too much or too little, and despite your best efforts, you could kill it in the end.

All the best intentions.

Back then, the day Charlie and his bride-to-be had stopped at Rosenbaum's for wedding bands, they thought what they had was something permanent. That it was special. That they had made a kind of greenhouse, by being together—a greenhouse where the bloom of new love would never die.

They did not know that when people looked at them, they were not marveling at their unique love. They were only daydreaming of the time before their own love had begun to require work—pruning and maintenance and protection from frost. A time before *they* knew firsthand that the bloom of love could wither despite their best efforts.

Charlie and his wife still had love. No longer quite so delicate and tender, but love just the same.

And he knew—he knew how easily daily life could poison it.

So here Charlie was, a man who had learned some of the hard lessons in life, a man who knew the weight of his own regrets. And he braced himself to hear some of Rosenbaum's hardest lessons. He had to, what with the jeweler looking at him now like he had himself been through something depleting. Like he had been drained. Far thinner than he had been the day Charlie and his wife bought their rings. Rougher.

"She brought me something. Something I didn't even realize was missing." Mr. Rosenbaum turned his left wrist over, tender side up. And he unfastened a wristwatch.

"It started out life as a small pocket watch," he explained, holding it out for Charlie to take. "I put a band on it because I was afraid of it getting lost again."

"You misplaced it once?"

"The watch didn't belong to me originally. Look at the engraving."

Charlie turned the watch over. He squinted and moved the watch closer to his nose and farther away again, trying to focus. The engraving was faint, barely there—like a cemetery headstone that had been worn nearly flat by weather.

"The first name," Charlie said.

"My grandfather," Irving said. "He told me a story when I was a boy. He said he had lost everything. Had hit a bad stretch. We all like to say times are hard now, and they are. But hard times can pop up anytime, find us anywhere. My grandfather had lost his business, his wife. Life felt like a high wire act. He had tumbled and there was no getting back up on it. That's how he described that time to me."

Irving's face grew less weary—younger, even, as he thought back to being a boy with his grandfather, listening to his tales.

"He told me an angel had rescued him. That she gave him gold coins and in return, all he had to give her was time." He smiled, shaking his head. "It seemed like a fairy tale to me. Jack and the magic beans."

Charlie couldn't move. His legs had grown heavy.

"She knocked on my door, this woman with the cloak, and she handed me that watch. She said my grandfather had needed help and he had found it. That he had once exchanged this watch for a loan. It was how he got back on his feet. Why he was able to open this shop. The same shop where my father worked. The shop where I work now."

"This business is part of your family," Charlie noted. "It's why you added the eyeglasses."

"I can't let this place go. Not after all these years. I think to people when they shop, a business is a convenience or a necessity. A place you go when you need it, every once in a while. When it's your own business, it's your soul."

Charlie nodded, feeling stabbed as he thought of Herman, sweating through the loss of his restaurant—the same establishment tainted with the history of the speakeasy that had once been on Charlie's beat.

"She told me someone might be coming in with a ring. Big and green and gaudy and worthless."

"She described it to you?"

"No, she *showed* it to me. Had it right there with her. Said I had to see it so I would know what to look for. She told me to tell the woman who would bring it by that it was real. That it was special. I was supposed to tell her to put it away for a rainy day. That it would save her, just as that exchanging of a gold watch had saved my grandfather."

"That's what you did out on the sidewalk," Charlie said. "What you told Mrs. Rossi."

"Yes."

"Why say something different inside the shop, though? You started talking about it being costume."

"Because I could tell people were listening in. I didn't want anyone to think Mrs. Rossi had something worth stealing. The last thing I'd want to be is the reason for a break-in."

So Irving had not been up to anything illegal—dishonest, perhaps, but not illegal. Charlie's nervous knots unwound a little.

"Didn't you ask the woman in the cloak to explain why she wanted you to do this?" Charlie said. "Lie to the Rossis?"

"Not lie. Stretch the truth."

"Semantics," Charlie corrected. "You didn't ask her?"

"You have to understand that I was so…discombobulated," Irving insisted. "There she was, with a piece of my family history, telling me this strange story. She was giving me back a piece of our past. Calling my grandfather by his first name, like she knew him. And she was telling me to promise to play along when someone came in with a worthless ring. And then she was gone. And there I was with my grandfather's watch."

Charlie stood there, the watch growing ever heavier in his fingers.

"I finally understood Grandfather's story," Irving said. "He traded that watch for money. Turned his *time* into *gold coins*. See? That's what he meant. He used the money to open this shop. This shop has been everything. It was my father's life. As a boy, it bought my shoes and groceries and…the first thing he ever sold was watches. Did you know that?"

Charlie shook his head.

"One of my most popular items. Stopwatches for conductors who ride the train. Even still, I think of my father and grandfather when I hear the train whistle as it pulls into the Sullivan depot."

"I should warn them. The Rossis, I mean," Charlie said.

"No—you can't. That's why I told you this story. To keep you from telling them."

"You don't want me to warn them that it has no value? They could make some foolish decisions, decisions about their money, believing that they have this ring as backup."

"But what is backup, Officer Barister? What if it's not money at all, but belief—enough belief to take a chance? That's what my grandfather got in the exchange, more than anything. He got money, sure. But he also got the strength to keep going. That was backup, too. What if having that ring gives the Rossis the strength to keep going, to believe, to know they'll be okay? What if backup is *hope*?"

Charlie handed Irving's watch over. And he turned for the door.

"What are you going to do?" Irving called.

"I don't know," Charlie said. And he meant it.

"IT'S A MIRROR," PETEY said, watching Walter pull the shiny object out from under the bush.

"How did it get there?" Petey asked. He might have offered a joke—something rough about Walter's mother, maybe, or the bush needing to doll itself up for a night on the town. But some silly old mirror—even one found, inexplicably, in a bush—paled in the space beside Petey's wish. He wanted that miserable Saturday of his to be good for *something*. And the something that he thought would be most satisfying was to get back at Bonwit for chasing after him earlier. It hadn't been enough for him to kick her mailbox off the railing. He wanted to truly get even. Then he would feel as though his Saturday hadn't been a complete waste.

"Come on, Walt," Petey insisted. "Come with me. Let's teach that old witch a lesson."

Walter was transfixed by the mirror—a graying pale metal, cold as ice from the hours in the snow. The glass of the mirror had worn along the edges, with black backing poking through.

When Walter turned the mirror over in his hands, it caught the late afternoon light and tossed it onto Petey's face.

Walter laughed. "It's why she looked like she glowed," he said. "Probably the light from the house bouncing off it."

"Why *who* glowed?" Petey asked, beginning to lose patience.

"The woman," Walter said, his tone laced with the kind of annoyance that said it should have all been perfectly clear to Petey by that point.

"What did you guys really do today, anyway? You and the cop?" Petey wanted to know.

But Walter didn't want to answer. Petey would tease him about the way he'd let the old woman go in the woods. *Jiminy Cricket,* he would swear at him, the same way he'd sworn at Walter for not walking the stretch beside Bonwit house the day before Thanksgiving.

From somewhere deep inside the Drummond house, Walter's mother called out to him.

The front door flapped open and she thundered outside. "*Walter,*" she shouted. "I told you—"

But she changed course as soon as she saw him standing there in her bushes, a mirror in his hand.

"Have you lost your mind?" she asked, stomping closer. "What is this?" She snatched the mirror away.

Once it was in her hand, her face shifted. The lines disappeared between her brows.

30.

TWILIGHT ENCROACHED ON THE Sullivan horizon as Charlie started his Chevy again and pulled away from the jewelry shop. This woman in the black cloak had definite ties to the town. Long-standing. She had to, didn't she, if she knew the Rosenbaum story? If she had his watch? *Why* would she have the watch? Regardless, Charlie thought, the woman had gnarly roots as deep as those from one of the hundred-year-old oaks that filled the park a mile from the business district. The same park where generations of children had played, the music of their laughter remaining constant even as the faces changed.

Charlie had himself played there—mumblety-peg and baseball, while the girls played jacks and hopscotch.

Had this woman played there as well? Had her children? How could so many people in town see her and not recognize her?

He passed by the Pendleton property, the ornate main house appearing to keep guard over the still pond. He hoped to catch Ida on her way home. Her annoyance with him earlier still stung. He wanted to erase her frown. Perhaps she had seen the woman.

Light through the downstairs windows cast colored rectangles across the snow-covered porch. The Pendletons who still lived there were in the midst of one of Ida's dinners. Her giant pies.

He could ring the bell. He really needed to ring the bell.

But he would interrupt them all.

Then again, he didn't *have* to ring the bell, he told himself. There was another option. That time of day, the Pendletons—and Ida—really would be too involved with supper to be looking out the windows. And even if they did happen to glance outside, the encroaching nightfall would conceal him. He could take a look at that ice house for himself, no one suspecting anything.

It wasn't right—in fact, the starch in Charlie's collar reminded him, he could very well be fired for this idea.

Charlie pulled the patrol car to a stop near the curb. His own shift should be over. His own dinner would be growing cold.

Charlie drummed his fingers on the top of the steering wheel.

And before he could question it, he was cutting the engine. Turning off his headlights.

Under the cover of encroaching darkness, he raced on foot through the snow, back to the ice house.

But he stopped beside the Pendletons' kitchen door, the snow beginning to fall again, when he found himself staring straight into a familiar face.

"Hello, Charlie," Ida said.

“IDA,” CHARLIE GREETED, TRYING on a smile.

Ida crossed her arms over her chest, anger written in the lines on her face.

“I see you found Bernard,” Charlie went on, nodding once at the man behind her shoulder.

“You don’t seem to trust that partner of yours too much,” Ida grumbled.

“Partner?” Charlie parroted.

“That little boy you had with you earlier. He told you there wasn’t a thing for you in that ice house.”

“I was coming to look for you,” Charlie lied.

“No, you weren’t,” Ida said, her voice little more than a whisper. But Charlie could hear her. She knew that.

She and Charlie were the kind of souls who had been so intertwined for so long, they’d wound up overlapping a bit. His thoughts and hers—her memories and his. They were two songs that played together to make a new one. Like all that fancy jazz improv that Dorothy and her husband used to play at Frankie's.

Ida slipped her hand inside the pocket of her cardigan, relieved to feel the gun and the piece of paper she had retrieved from the ice house. She knew that Charlie could only see part of the picture. And she wasn't about to let the rest come out. Not if Bernard wanted it kept quiet. Not if Bernard thought it was a precious thing that needed protecting. Ida loved Charlie. But there was a line between him and her friend Bernard. And that line was as big as the world.

"I wanted to talk to you real quick, before you had to get back to the Pendletons," Charlie said.

"I already served those Pendletons. Old man Pendleton likes to eat earlier and earlier these days." She narrowed her eyes.

"I have to get to the bottom of this," Charlie finally admitted. "I can't let somebody get hurt. Not again. Not on my watch."

"I was there, too, that night, Charlie. Not for the bullets, but before. You think I ain't got guilt in me? But Charlie, putting more people in jail isn't going to help a thing."

"I don't want to put anyone away—"

"Yes, you do," Ida scolded. "You do—and I'm telling you, there's no way you're ever going to lock up your bad feelings. Those'll be with you till you die. You can't fix something that's already come and gone, Charlie. You can't forget it, either. Can't lock it up in some cage and think it'll fade once you don't have to look at it. I knew the people in this town would be sorry for giving you that fancy new car. Fancy new shortwave. It's not a thank-you for doing good work, Charlie. It's the hope that you'll have something you can rely on so you might relax a little."

"That's not it—" Charlie tried to interrupt.

Ida tugged her hand from her cardigan and she started to

shake her finger at him. What happened next was maybe another magical ingredient. Hetty would certainly think of it that way in later years. Right then, right at that moment, to Ida? It felt like the worst thing that could happen. Because tugging her hand from her pocket that quickly had dislodged the list Ida had picked up in the ice house. It hit the air and it fluttered in the cold right beside the small snow-flakes, the ones that swirled and hovered and never seemed to quite get anywhere.

Ida gasped and pawed at the air, trying to claw that list back.

Charlie snatched it up first, though.

Under the harsh stare of his flashlight, Charlie found an aged feminine script—shaky cursive handwriting. A list: Mr. Rosenbaum's pocket watch. A pearl from an old necklace to return to Rose who worked the switchboard at the phone company. A letter opener to return to James at the drug store.

The list continued, the script purposefully tiny in order to get it all to fit, running onto both sides of the page. A good number of the items had been crossed off, but two that had not stood out: *Ring for the Rossis* and, Charlie was horrified to see, *the speakeasy.*

That was how it had been written—*the speakeasy.* Not Her-man's restaurant. Or even Frankie's old place.

"What does this mean?" Charlie asked, pointing. "Did she leave this out here? The woman in the cloak?"

"Charlie, you can't—" Ida tried.

"Does she know about that Christmas Eve all those years ago? How?"

This was it, Charlie thought. It was everything, right here, about to be revealed—it was Herman's case—and the kind of town Sullivan was going to be—and his son's entire childhood.

It was Charlie, too. It was that young man he had once been, winking at the girls, leaning on streetlights.

"This whole thing is about the speakeasy, isn't it?" Charlie asked. "The woman in the cloak—this is her list. And everything comes together somehow at the speakeasy."

"Charlie," Ida tried again, "you need to do your old Ida a favor. You need to tell her you're going home to that pretty wife and that baby of yours."

"I can't, Ida. I can't."

"You will."

"I have to make things right," Charlie insisted, and he began to run.

"I'm so sorry, Bernard," Ida said as Charlie grew smaller. "I shouldn't have let him get his hands on that list. I should have done something before now. I thought for sure after Charlie chased her away, Hetty was headed straight for home."

"I think he's right," Bernard said. "I think she *is* at the speakeasy. I think if Hetty has any breath in her body, she's looking for Gent's music box."

"Come on, then," Hetty said. "We'd better do our best to beat Charlie there."

32.

ONE OF THE BEAUTIFUL things about a music box was how much it could teach a person about interconnectedness. Or so Gent used to tell Hetty.

Those spinning wheels and gears inside, the little bumps that could replicate specific tones of the scale—why, they all depended on one another. One little gear falters and nothing works.

A lock, or so Hetty had discovered long ago, also functioned in the same way. Why, she was the best lock picker that side of the Mississippi—or so Gent had said, with a kind of devilish grin.

Sometimes—not often, but sometimes—knowing how to pick a lock was important. It all depended on who, exactly, was in that carriage house out back. How deep their despair. More than once, Hetty had been forced to pick that lock, rouse the tenant from their bed.

"No room here for melancholy," she would inform them.

The carriage house was no place for a person to simply hide

from the world. Sometimes, a forced scrubbing and a good meal and exposure to sunlight was all a person needed.

That "guest house," as Gent had sometimes called their carriage house, did not have a one-hundred-percent success rate. But it was high. Ninety-seven, maybe? Who knew for sure. Gent and Hetty did not keep score.

Maybe it was foolish to only have one key, that being the one their guest received. But Gent and Hetty were the sort who wanted to trust. The same way other people wanted a second piece of pie at the diner. It was their knew-better pleasure. One that occasionally hit them with a different sort of heartburn.

Hetty's proficiency in lock picking was with her still that evening, in that alley behind Herman's closed restaurant, even with her knobby fingers and the eyesight that was getting more and more like a pinhole, requiring more and more light.

What good was light anyway, when picking a lock? It wasn't about sight. It was about feel. Like dancing, really.

And so she stood there, under her cloak, in the alley. And she removed her own set of tools, modified from a set of Gent's delicate music box repair tools. Small screwdrivers and tweezers and the like. And she set to work.

The door squeaked open, and Hetty smiled—just as she'd smiled every night she'd opened that door for herself and Bernard. But the surge brought by her success lasted only a moment. Because as soon as she began to step inside, it hit her that Bernard was not there to follow her. Bad feelings and second thoughts caught up to her again.

Bernard would be worried. Frantic, most likely. She hated making him feel that way. There was no joy in that. She did not want to hurt her one remaining friend.

But the Rossis' back door had actually been closer to Frankie's old place than her home. It was going to take her so long to get anywhere, what with all the stops to rest along the way. Why go home when she could go straight to the speakeasy?

Need had overtaken her. She had not been able to resist. She had not been able to keep herself from Frankie's alley door.

And the music box. Gent's box. It had to be inside. Her unsuccessful search so far had not discouraged her.

Gent was a romantic, maybe. But not a ne'er-do-well. Never that. If there was something about that music box that would save her, Gent had meant that literally. Why else would he need Bernard to take it to the bank?

She moved cautiously into the building, the interior darker even than the alley. She held her hand out in front of her, trying to find out if she was about to bump into anything.

Shame overtook her. This was foolish. It was so dark inside. Previous nights, Bernard had brought along the kerosene lantern that had always hung on the Bonwit back door. The one that had always offered them a bit of light should a nighttime sound need investigating. Now, she had no light at all. How would she ever find the music box that way?

Hetty stopped walking. Shook her head at herself. This trip was useless. She should have gone home. Gotten Bernard. What had she been thinking?

"*Hetty*," she scolded herself.

Until a light popped to life. Up by the bar.

She sighed. "Bernard," she said. "You came without me, you scoundrel."

When he didn't answer, she continued, "You know your Hetty, don't you? You knew I'd be here. You knew to come."

She shuffled up to the bar, but there was no one. Not yet. "Bernard?" she called. "Where are you? Have you found any sign of the music box yet?"

She placed a hand on the edge of the bar, her chest tight. "I'll check behind the bar again myself if I can rest here for a moment."

But the barstool was higher than she remembered. Then again, she hadn't sat at the bar last time, had she? There were still some tables, left over from Frankie's day. Tables and chairs. All stacked up, in storage. Bernard had pulled out a chair for her. Given her some boxes to sort through.

She let out a high-pitched "Whooooooo," as she realized how hard she would have to work to hoist herself into the seat. "I'll need some help, Bernard. Bernard?"

A thunk on the bar drew her eye.

And there it was. Just like that. As though it had been plunked down from the heavens.

"The music box," Hetty breathed, relief cascading down her arms and legs. "Oh, Bernard, I knew we could find it."

A hand came to rest on her own.

Hetty's eyes traveled up the man's arm, all the way to his face.

But that wasn't Bernard looking at her.

It was her beloved Gent.

33.

GENT SMILED AT HER—that lovely smile of his that had always seemed to Hetty like both a warm welcome and a feeling of having been home for a long time, even the very first time she saw him. He wore his favorite suit, the one he'd had for years, the same he'd had on the snowy December day he'd brought Bernard from the train station.

"I've been working some time now to keep this safe," he said, pushing the music box closer to her.

"You?" Hetty asked. "You?" What she meant was, *How can this be? How can you be standing here, right in front of me?*

"I learned soon after leaving you that my box had not been taken to the bank, as I'd wanted," Gent said. He leaned closer to her, propping his elbows on the bar. "Not that I—" He frowned, looking deep into her eyes. "My dear. You look absolutely faint."

Before Hetty could understand what was happening, she was sitting on the barstool. And she had a glass in front of her.

"A bit of ginger ale," he told her. "You're looking a bit worse for the wear, I'm afraid. Might I get you anything else?"

How many times had she seen that exact look of concern on his face? How was it that she was seeing it at that moment?

"What has happened to me?" she asked. Trembling, unable to swallow, she asked, "Have I—did I—" She reached up to touch her face. "Did I die?"

"Oh, dear, no," Gent said, taking her hand.

Hetty's eyes swelled as she looked down at their fingers, intertwined yet again. "How is it that I can feel you?" she whispered.

"Now, you know me. You know that I would never simply leave you without making sure you were taken care of. I'm sorry that this all took so very long. That you had to sell so many precious things."

"You know?" she asked. Then, a dark cloud passing all the way through her, "You know." Meaning, he knew about her behavior. The horrible way she'd treated everyone.

But Gent, in his tender way, only said, "I know how important it is to you to return those items I saved."

The building pressure of Hetty's shame began to let go. A tight grip had been pried away. "Yes," she agreed. "It is."

"Imagine, then, how important it has been for me to see you here. And how relieved I am to know that you will have this." He nudged the music box.

"Why now?" Hetty asked. "I've been here before."

"But not alone," Gent told her.

"What difference would it have made?" Hetty asked. She had never questioned Gent before. But she could not even be certain this was Gent. It couldn't have been. What was she looking at? A ghost? A mirage?

Her eyes stung. Her mouth was painfully dry. Words had grit

and scraped her throat.

She gripped the glass of ginger ale. It was cold. Ice chips float-ed on the top. How was it possible to still have ice in the building? Herman's restaurant had been closed for weeks.

"You gave the box to Bernard. I was with Bernard. Why do I now have to be alone?" Hetty asked.

"The heart finds it easier to trust when the outside world is gone," Gent told her. And pushed the box still closer.

"I knew it," she whispered. "I knew you would make sure I had this. If it was truly important. I knew you'd find a way."

Hetty stared at it a moment, that delicate work of Gent's. What an artist he was, what a sculptor he had been. Her shaky hand reached for the box, her large blue veins popping up against her nearly translucent skin. The hinge cracked a bit as it moved.

Inside, she found a sheet of paper.

"Oh, my," she said, holding the page far enough away to read the type. "Oh, my."

The type blurred as her eyes welled. "And you've been here all alone, keeping this for me," Hetty said.

"We all have," Gent corrected.

"We who?"

"Everyone who comes for happy hour," Gent said.

"This can't be real," Hetty said, laughing. "I want it to be, but—it can't."

"I suppose," Gent said, "that the only way to prove it to you is show you."

He walked to the far wall and clicked on the light. When Hetty glanced behind her, she found the room was full. And as soon as she saw it, she heard it. Music pouring from the piano. Glasses clinking. Voices shouting. Feet stomping the floor.

Gent swept her off the stool and into his arms.

Suddenly, they were dancing.

Of all things. In Gent's arms, she had the energy of her youth. She could have danced all night. Spinning about the room didn't bother her. She wasn't dizzy. Love was here. She had found her Gent. And everything was just as Hetty remembered.

34.

CHARLIE THREW HIS PATROL car into park and bolted for the entrance to Herman's restaurant.

It was night by then. Night came early, there, in December. Stars glittered over Charlie's head as he banged on the entrance.

"Herman!" he shouted.

Snow swirled in front of his face, the flakes spaced far apart. For the second time that day, he cupped his hands around his eyes and tried to peer through the plate glass, in-between the painted "Puddin's" sign. "Herman?"

But no one answered. Yet again. The inside was darker even than the night. Why wouldn't Herman be here? If Charlie had been renting this place, and had some idea that it had been broken into the night before, you could bet Charlie would be there now. Probably spend the night.

But he wouldn't be out front, in the old restaurant, he reminded himself. He'd be keeping watch on that alley door.

Charlie raced around the building, straight for the familiar alley.

Could secrets hum? Almost like electric lights? It seemed to Charlie the air in the alley pulsed. The strange woman—the refusal of Sullivan to talk about her—the list in the ice house—it all added up to something. But what?

At that moment, Charlie was convinced he was about to find out. He would crack open the truth of the old woman in the black cloak.

Afterward, the town would be different. They would smile when he approached them at the newsstand, because they would know that this time, he had saved them.

Christmas would come, like a present they could all unwrap together, shiny with promise.

They would celebrate together. Charlie's own childhood would come back to him, and he would pass it to Tom like the heirloom he'd wanted it to be.

So sure of success, it didn't not occur to him to question why the usually bolted back door was cracked open.

With no hesitation, Charlie stepped inside.

"Herman?" he called.

But his voice was drowned out by the sound of a trumpet.

35.

A TRUMPET BLARED IN Charlie's ears—so loud, it felt as though the music was being played inches from his head.

Dorothy's voice soared. Couples swirled arm-in-arm around Charlie.

Frankie walked by, pausing to wink at him. "Never thought you'd get here," she told him. "And here it is Christmas Eve."

"Christmas—Eve?" Charlie croaked, sure that Frankie would never be able to hear him over the music.

"Sure. You told me you had a Christmas party to go to. I knew you'd never cut me out of Christmas, though." She started to walk away, a pitcher of martinis in her hand.

But she stopped, pointed at Charlie and addressed him in a tone not unlike the schoolteachers who had scolded Charlie for his boyish behavior. "You'd better promise me you'll be here for New Year's. I don't want this place to ring in 1932 without you."

"193—2?" Charlie asked.

But it was already 1938.

Charlie's head swirled, spinning faster than the dancing couples. Before, simply being in the room had made his memories intensify. But this—it was real. So much more so than whatever had happened to him the last time he'd stepped inside. He could smell the candles burning on the tables. The food in the back room. Perfume. Piano chords joined with the trumpet already vibrating in his chest. A dull, unexpected pain exploded against his back. He turned to hear, "Sorry, Charlie, didn't mean to bump you," from a dancer who quickly dissolved into drunken laughter and led his partner away.

This was it. This was the night he had regretted for the last seven years. The Christmas Eve of the shootout, come back to life.

Yes, here it all was—just as it had been in 1931, decked out for the holiday. The room was full of people. Dancing. Singing. Glasses clinking. Laughter roaring. Frankie circling the room. Edna, the bartender, leaned against the giant carved ornate bar, talking animatedly to her brother-in-law, one of the many regulars that Frankie said kept the place afloat.

Music soared, drawing Charlie still deeper into the night. And there they were, at the piano: Dorothy the songbird, draped over the piano. And her husband at her side, his trumpet singing harmony with her.

Charlie began to formulate a plan. If the past was back, that meant that he could stop this, right? He could stop everything from happening? The shootout?

Desperation exploded through his chest. This was it—the thing he had wanted more than anything. Years had passed, and still, the intensity of the wish to go back had not lessened. He had assumed he would carry it with him the rest of his life.

But here, now—a chance. All he had ever wanted. Like the

most miraculous Christmas gift, it was here.

He took a step toward the back door. In the alley, he could meet up with the cops who had raided the speakeasy and keep them from busting in, weapons drawn. Maybe, he thought, his head a confused swarm, he could never stop the arrests. Not now, not this late. But surely he could stop the shooting. People getting hurt.

He found himself being pushed by the twirling couples, turned suddenly in the wrong direction.

He tried another step in the direction of the alley door.

And the couples twirled him in the wrong direction again.

Each time he tried, they turned him, twirled him, sent him farther away. No matter which direction he tried weaving through the crowd, he couldn't manage to get out of the room.

The past was a whirlpool swirling about him, inescapable. The same scene over and over, and no chance to get to the place he needed to be to change anything.

How could this be? Was he being denied again? It was pure torture to be here, to know that he had done wrong before, to know what he needed to do now and not be able to get there—to have the ending that he had wished for be an inch from his fingertips and find himself unable to grasp it.

Until a woman grabbed his arm—an older woman. No one he remembered from those speakeasy days.

Charlie felt certain he had seen that face, though. It was hazy, but—

Who was that?

"I told him he would change his mind if he came," she said, offering Charlie an *I-knew-it* kind of smirk.

Charlie didn't know who she was talking about, and he didn't care. He wanted out of the speakeasy. Into the alley. To change everything. Maybe the woman, standing rooted there, could block the other dancers long enough for Charlie to slip out.

"Gent loaned Frankie the money when her restaurant started to flounder. Well. Not loaned. Gave. In exchange for that derringer of hers, the one that no longer had a hammer." The woman's wrinkles deepened as she smiled. "Of course, it would be hard to part with that gun if you kept it in your garter as a protection. Folks are always afraid enough of a gun that they never do look close enough to find out if it could, in fact, still shoot them." She laughed.

"Are you—Mrs. Bonwit?" he asked.

"Hetty, please," she said. "We don't cross paths too often, do we, Officer Barister?"

"No," he said. "We don't."

"Well, I'll tell you something. Gent was practically beside himself when he heard that Frankie had opened a speakeasy with our money. I said maybe we ought to give it a look. Maybe then it wouldn't seem so bad."

"What does he think now?" Charlie asked.

Hetty laughed again and turned her shoulder enough for Charlie to see a white-headed man at the piano, a crystal glass of something brown in his hand, singing along to "Up On the Housetop."

"I have to go," Charlie told her.

"Where?" Hetty asked.

"If I can't go out the back, I should go out the front. Maybe I can still beat them," Charlie said, but Hetty wouldn't let go of him.

"They blocked that entrance, you know."

"Who?"

"Some of the boys here. To give us more time."

"That makes no sense," Charlie insisted. "I have to go."

"Where?" Hetty repeated. And shrugged.

In that same instant, the entire room emptied. No more people, no more music.

The furniture was all still there, but stacked and pushed to the side. The room was filled with boxes. A single light shone up by the bar—but no bartender. The silence—a stark contrast to the boisterous Christmas Eve party of a moment ago—smacked against Charlie's ears.

He had no idea what had just happened to him. He only knew one thing:

He and Hetty Bonwit were the only two left inside.

36.

"WHERE DID YOU GET this?" Walter's mother asked, turning the mirror over in her hands.

"What is it?" Walter felt the embarrassment of such a ridiculous question.

"It was my mother's," Mrs. Drummond said, knowing what he meant. "My—father gave it to her, I think. She had this hair—beautiful hair, always brushing it. And he gave it to her. It was nothing fancy. But it meant something to her. Especially after he died."

Her eyes grew distant. She was reliving it. Almost as though she could watch it all play out again in that mirror.

"She sold it," Walter's mother said, her voice softer.

"The mirror?" Walter asked, but his mother was far enough away in her memory by then that she didn't even hear him.

"I remember, she took me with her. To the funeral parlor. I don't know why—of all the girls. Maybe because I was the youngest. But I remember, she broke down. I'd never seen her that way, and it scared me. It's terrifying to see the person you depend on fall apart."

She tilted the mirror, throwing the light about. "I can see Petey's grandfather still. Telling her to take something. To sell it, I think. Or—get money for it. I don't know where. Someone—someone in town. I remember my mother saying we didn't have anything. He told her, he said to take something that *mattered*. She took her mirror. And right after that, we all wound up with work. All of us. Mother and me and every one of my sisters."

"Aunt Lilith, who hand-cranked the neighbor's car," Walter said.

"Yes," his mother said, pleased he had remembered her stories. "I know it was all his doing. The man she took her mirror to. But I don't know who. It didn't matter to me. My father was gone. And she—and my sisters—they were working. Like it didn't bother them. I couldn't understand it. I was hurting. Why weren't they? My mother said—she said—there was no time to be sad. She told me not to be—to be—" Her voice crumbled. She couldn't admit the rest.

"A tenderheart," Walter finished.

37.

"**I**T'S YOU," CHARLIE STAMMERED, staring into Hetty's face.

"Of course," she said. And smiled. Hetty didn't think Charlie had any idea how true those simple words really were. It *was* her. Gent had mere seconds ago been right there (the thrill had not left her yet—*Gent had taken her into his arms!*), and in his embrace, she had come back to herself. To her old self, that shy girl with the red hair who had hated parties but had loved one man fiercely. She was not gone for good. That girl she had once been was itself a trinket that Gent had brought back. And even now that Gent had faded yet again, Hetty could still feel her, right there, underneath the rusty hinges. Recognizable to anyone who bothered to really look.

"I was so lost there for a moment," Charlie admitted. "In my own—"

"—memories," Hetty finished.

"Wishes," Charlie corrected. He tried to make his face neutral, though. Tried to pretend that it had not dented his heart to find himself here, with her alone, with the night of his greatest regret gone again.

And no way to fix it.

"They seem more alive to you in here, do they?" Hetty asked, dragging herself toward the bar. She used the edge to steady herself. Before Charlie could get his thoughts together, realizing he should help her onto a stool, she had already hoisted herself onto one. She wasn't going to wait for help. Not now, not after her visit with Gent. She wiggled back and forth, finding a comfortable spot on Ida's old stool—the one Frankie had reserved for Sullivan's own five-star chef.

Somehow, the dancing and the boisterous speakeasy—and Gent and the music box—it had strengthened her. The things he had whispered in her ear as they'd danced—the truth about his music box—had sharpened her own plan. It was now a pencil ready to write the last remaining paragraphs.

But she needed Charlie to help her. It had to be Charlie, because he already had so many ties to Frankie's old speakeasy, to the past, to Sullivan. The past had come to life for him—every bit as vividly as it had for Hetty—so great was his desire to get back to a Sullivan he had known before. Before the raid, before the Depression, before he grew up.

Hetty patted the seat of the barstool beside her, not realizing it had always been Charlie's, the one he'd sat on when the speakeasy was still in business.

But she saw how reluctant Charlie was to sit on it.

"Still have some bad feelings about the place, Charlie? I never did myself, not even when it was still Frankie's speakeasy. Came once, with Gent. He was the one who was hesitant. So much so, I began to regret suggesting we'd come. At least, until Gent started having such a good time. Then I completely relaxed into it. I hadn't seen him have that much fun in ages. It turned into one of my favorite memories. In fact, I was reliving it myself."

"You were?"

"Yes, I was."

"Were you here on Christmas Eve? The last Christmas Eve?"

"No. Not then."

"I was thinking of it—"

"But you weren't here, either. Not that night."

"No, ma'am," Charlie said.

"Well, memories appear to have a tendency to get a bit tangled up in here."

Charlie finally slid onto the barstool, in order to look Hetty in the eye.

"How did you get in here?" Charlie wanted to know.

Hetty pushed an ornately-carved music box down the bar. "I was looking for this," she said, sidestepping the question of her breaking in. "Gent left it for me. Bernard—he *was* here the night of the raid. A few hours before. Accidentally left it behind. I've only been coming to find this thing that was mine. You have to know that it's mine by looking at it. Gent and his music boxes," she said wistfully, running a knobby finger across the carved detail.

"So *you* were the one getting in here." He could feel the knot of the unknown begin to unwind. No one from the Hooverville, no fires—just an old woman.

"I didn't break anything or disturb anything. Did I?"

"Still. You can't break and enter—"

"And it was only to retrieve what was mine."

Charlie sighed. "And this time, you found it? You can stop coming in now?"

"This time, Gent brought it to me," Hetty corrected.

Had he? Really? Charlie had himself seen Gent. But then again, it couldn't be. Reason had found him again. "Now, Mrs. Bonwit—"

"All I have to do is begin to crack this music box open and I can hear music. Even though it's been broken for years." Hetty's hand shook as she opened the box—maybe half an inch.

"I'm sorry, Mrs. Bonwit. I don't hear—I'm not saying you don't—"

"But you saw the speakeasy as it once was. A mere moment ago."

"I don't know what that was."

"Almost as though it was real. So strong was the memory."

Charlie began to wonder how it could be possible for two people to have the same memory. But he couldn't ask. Was afraid to ask. Knots were beginning to tighten up inside of him again. Did he want what he had seen to be real or not? How did it change his idea of the place—of Hetty—of Sullivan? He wasn't sure. But he knew that he couldn't lie to Hetty. "Yes," he agreed. "It was real."

"Is your wish to make things different, Officer Barister?"

"Yes," he whispered. "I would very much like to make things different."

She brightened. "I had hoped so."

"Are you aware that Gent was quite the benefactor in Sullivan?" she asked.

"Yes. I am."

"You are, it seems, one of the few."

"Is that what you would like to change, Mrs. Bonwit?" he asked.

"In a way."

"I would think you'd be quite angry at Sullivan. For their forgetting. That you would resent it."

"My recent behavior has not been fueled by anger, officer. It's been fueled by fear of losing what little is left."

"Part of you must regret—at least a little—giving to a town who then turned from you. Took and took, and when you needed something in return, they didn't give back."

"But they did give back, officer. So many of them. The repayment was seeing so many people in Sullivan get back on their feet."

"Still, though—here you are, monetarily hurting."

"Ah, but we did get paid back. By one of them, anyway."

"Only one? That might still make me angry."

"It's a big one. One that makes up for everything."

She smiled at the music box. "As it turns out, there was a reason that Gent wanted me to have this. Why he told Bernard that I would be saved by this box if hard times came to call. This music box, in a way, is my carriage house."

Hetty opened it all the way, exposing a piece of folded paper, the top clearly marked, "Warranty Deed." She handed the paper to Charlie.

"This is for this building," Charlie said, his voice high-pitched with surprise. "Frankie's place. The city's been everywhere looking for it."

"Frankie apparently left it with Gent. As a thank-you. Because Gent was the one who rescued this place when times got bad for Frankie. In case anything ever happened to Frankie, Gent—and I— would have this place to fall back on."

"This building belongs to you," Charlie said.

"It does," Hetty said.

"You can sell it," Charlie said, brightening. Perhaps this would ease Hetty's troubles. Bring an end to her ongoing quarrel with her neighborhood.

"Of course not."

"Now, Hetty, you can't spend the rest of your life on mere scraps. You can't—" But she was already shaking her head, telling him he was wrong.

"I won't need it." She spoke with a calm assurance.

"Hetty, you're worrying me a bit."

"Oh, please. I'm an old woman. I'm well aware of how my body's winding down."

"You can't know for certain, though."

"Spoken like a man with plenty of time on his hands," she said.

They stared at each other.

"I want you to file that deed with the recorder's office," Hetty told him. "I want the city to continue to manage it. And I want only the right person to buy it. The kind of person my own Gent would have wanted to have it. A good soul, maybe one a little worse for the wear. Someone needing a direction. A love. Someone whose ways would keep the same spirit of the place alive."

"How will the city know who that is?"

"This building will tell them." Hetty raised a finger to make sure that Charlie would not argue with this.

Charlie leaned back. He didn't believe her. Not yet, anyway. Even after all he had seen inside the old speakeasy.

Hetty only marveled at it—at the way that everyone always spoke of the wisdom that came with age, all while immediately discounting people arthritic and white-haired, thinking of them all as muddled and bewildered. Foggy at best.

So she said, "I believe you would like to have a second shot at that Christmas Eve all those years ago. You would like to redeem yourself. Undo what you feel was your part in destroying this speakeasy. It is, in fact, a dream of yours."

Charlie wondered if anyone else in town knew this about him. "Yes," he admitted.

"What if I told you that you could have it—but only if you helped me finish my own plans?"

"You already told me. You want me to file the deed. Arrange for the city to continue to manage the property."

"Yes. I do. But it's more than that. I've been returning trinkets to their original owners. Items that were left with Gent in exchange for the help that was needed at the time."

"You stopped by Rosenbaum's on Thanksgiving. And the Drummond house."

"I did."

"And the Rossis. You set that whole thing up."

"Yes."

"So why the disguise?" Charlie asked. "Why sneak around? If you're simply returning items—"

"Because what I want to leave everyone with more than an old keepsake. I want them to know that in the midst of horrible times—gray, dead-end times in which it feels as though all you can do is drown over and over again—there is still something really kind about the world. And that kindness is magic. Because if they believe it, they'll *do* it. Do you see what I mean?"

"But—"

"I don't want my name associated with any of it," Hetty said, anticipating his next question. "My name is tainted, now, by the way I've acted since Gent died. I don't want them to think I'm buying their forgiveness. I don't even want forgiveness. What's done is done. What I want is for this town to feel like my house did, all those years. When it was Gent and Bernard and all those people who came—it wasn't sad, when they were there. It was so full of hope. There is nothing better than a new start, is there, Charlie? You know what I mean. You have a little boy."

Charlie only blinked at her, marveling at the fact that in the midst of everything happening to Hetty the last few years—the death of her husband and the loss of all the things that had been so important to her—she also knew about Tom.

Hetty only smiled at him. Why wouldn't she know about Tom? Why wouldn't she know about them all? There they all went, every day, traipsing past her windows.

"For the most part," Hetty said, "I've succeeded. And you, I trust, will take care of the deed. That leaves this music box. I have to get it in the right hands in the right way. In a way that will help someone believe in it."

"Believe in what?"

Hetty shook her head. "That's for the recipient to find out." The truth was that she had only just learned of it herself. From Gent, whispering in her ear on the dance floor.

"How would I do that?" Charlie asked, squinting at her. "Help someone believe in a broken music box?"

He was doing it again—considering her befuddled and confused.

But Hetty looked him square in the eye. "By getting Walter to my funeral."

Charlie's frown deepened. "What does that—"

"My music box—this same one my husband left for me, was the first he ever made. He put all his own dreams into this box. And it will be back in the vault at the bank. My housekeeper will return it, with specific instructions to our attorney. Walter will inherit it. This box is special, Charlie. That's why Gent put the deed in it. The box and instructions on how to use it will be given to the inheritor."

"You're writing Walter into your will?"

"No, I'm bequeathing this music box to whoever shows up at my funeral. Safe to say that no one will be coming. Not voluntarily. Not after the way I've treated everyone. But I do need one person to show. To inherit this box. And yes, I want it to be Walter."

"Why him?" Charlie sharpened his gaze at her. "Did he let you go on purpose? Out there behind the Pendleton home?"

"He didn't know it was me. He knew I was the same person who had been to his house. But he doesn't think that person is mean old Hetty Bonwit." She paused a beat, then explained, "We had a moment. Out at his house. A silly, kind moment together, when I tried to return something to the Drummonds. I saw him in the window, and I went up to him. To cheer him, and I—something was there, officer. Between the two of us. I kept myself hidden from him, with my cloak, and the way he was with a stranger…the way he's been trying to help me. He's different."

"His mother might have said something about that."

"He's a tenderheart," Hetty told him. "I've heard his mother call him that. I like the term. It's so much like my dear late husband. And, Charlie, just like you."

"I'm not, Mrs. Bonwit. I maybe was when I was younger. I'll give you that." He found himself ready to dismiss everything that he had felt and seen inside the old speakeasy. It was the word that did it: *tenderheart*. The last thing Charlie wanted to be. Having it pinned to him made him immediately retreat. "I learned the error of my ways," Charlie told her. "I'm sorry, but the only way to fix what happened seven years ago is to make sure it never happens again. To ensure that secrets are never allowed to fester."

Charlie's words crashed into Hetty with a weight far heavier even than the fatigue she'd felt out in the woods. "So that means you're going to expose me? To the whole town?"

"It means I'm going to tell Herman I know who's been coming in here. Tell him it's you."

"You can't do that, Charlie, please," Hetty begged, putting a hand on his. She could feel the world unraveling. Like rows and rows of knitting getting pulled free, a scratchy wool yarn zipping there against her palm. "You won't do it? Fulfill my request? About the music box?"

"I can't play games, Mrs. Bonwit. I can't let any more secrets take root here. I'm going to tell Herman, and I'm going to tell Mrs. Drummond who was at her house." He pointed to the cloak on the bar. "I'll tell the Rossis, too. Warn them that ring of theirs is worthless."

"Oh, but Charlie, no, no—"

In the back corner of the old speakeasy, something rustled. Almost like a bird's wings trying to flap to flight. It was all going to fly away. It was going to fall apart.

Hetty scrambled to grip him tighter. "It's so simple, Charlie. All I need—I need someone *official* to file that deed. No one will question it. Not if it's you, Charlie. The town *wants* to know what to do with this building. And then, all I ask is that you get Walter to my funeral. Bernard will take care of the rest. I think—why, I think the best way to get Walter to my funeral is through his best friend. Petey, isn't it? It couldn't be easier. Please, Charlie. Please. *That* will put Sullivan on the right path. Don't you see?"

Charlie straightened up. "Did you hear that?" he asked. "Is someone out front? Herman, maybe." He pulled himself from the barstool.

"No, Charlie—I have something here to convince you."

But such convincing didn't come in the form of even more words. More pleading. More making her case.

It came in the form of an old toy, cold to the touch—a piece of long-ago December that was pressed into his hand.

38.

CHARLIE HAD, IN FACT, heard someone outside the building. Two someones. He had heard Bernard and Ida, knocking on the door and calling his name.

"Charlie!" Ida shouted. "It's me!" How could he ignore her this way? Was he that angry at her for their exchanges by the ice house? It had to be that he didn't hear.

Bernard pounded the front window. The outdoor air was so cold that his knuckles stung as they rapped on the glass, every bit as much as they would if he were to knock on ice. What was he doing? How could he possibly be here, and not in the woods? Gent had said the box was important, would save her. But what if he and Ida had chosen wrong? What if there was no Hetty to save, because she had frozen out there in the woods? The later it got, the darker it got, and the less likely he would be to find her. Black cloak under a black sky. Had he really been that certain he would find Hetty here? Or had he been driven by his own guilt? Was he really here for a silly broken music box?

What was wrong with him? Bernard knocked louder, not feeling the pain that time.

Another vehicle pulled to a stop. The headlights glared at Bernard, knocking on the front window, and Ida, twisting the knob on the front door.

"What are you doing?" Herman asked, his voice carrying across the square before he had completely pulled himself from his Plymouth. He had been circling about, driving the streets along the square, looking—though he wasn't sure for what. Officer Barister to show up? Signs of anyone milling about in the dark? Somehow, it had seemed a better strategy than simply sitting inside his old restaurant.

And now, here, Officer Barister's car had appeared parked next to the curb, and Ida and Bernard were suddenly screaming and banging on the entrance. Carrying on like a couple of fools.

Herman began to sweat again.

Ida and Bernard did not look at each other.

"Were you two here before? Huh?" Herman asked.

Ida put her hand inside her coat pocket to touch the derringer. All she could do was hope she and Bernard were not looking at Herman in the way of children who had been caught misbehaving.

"Were you two here last night?" Herman asked. He was angry, but neither Bernard nor Ida exactly saw a monster. They saw a storm. A storm had no malice. A storm, just by existing, destroyed everything.

What would Herman see if he went inside? Hetty? Would her precious secret shatter?

"Herman, now, you know me," Ida started. "Me and—recipes. The Pendletons—you know, they have their big Christmas shindigs, and Old Ida's getting on in years. I can't handle those things all by myself anymore."

"This time of night you come to talk about this?"

"When else? I work all day. Bernard and I both work there, you know. We thought, though, since Charlie was here, he might help us get word to you. That's why we were calling out to him."

"Sure, you were," Herman grumbled, reaching for the front door.

"About the recipe, Herman. I need to talk about your Ozark Pudding. For the party."

"Oh, let's talk recipes," Herman growled. "How about the recipes you came up with for Frankie? You're the reason people kept coming back. Without that shootout, I might have had a chance with this place."

Ida squeezed the derringer. How many times had the world treated her like she was no different than that old useless gun, missing its hammer? No power to speak of, posing no danger to anyone. And how many times had Frankie laughed and told Ida, "We know better"?

"Now, Herman," Ida scolded, "if there'd been no shootout, you never would have been able to afford rent here. Now, I know how you are. Folks get mad, they try to hold it in, but that only lasts so long before it starts shooting out, as hard to keep control of as a fire hose. I know you're hurting because you lost your place, but I'm not the one…" She was rattling. She knew it. But there had to be a word in her someplace, tucked in some hidden crevice inside her, something that would delay Herman or turn him around. She had to protect Hetty. At first, her determination had all been for Bernard. But with that little piece of Frankie's place back in her pocket, it seemed bigger, some-how. That not-so-long-ago yesterday was calling out to her. Asking her to keep it safe.

It wasn't as though Ida thought Herman was unworthy of

Hetty's secret. She only knew that for Herman, there was no value in keeping that secret hidden.

Herman reached again for the door.

But the boys on the other side—some of those speakeasy regulars that Hetty had mentioned to Charlie—they were still there, on the other side of that door. They were putting everything they had against it, to keep that lock from turning.

They knew Hetty and Charlie needed just a little more time.

DEEP IN THE BUILDING, in the old speakeasy, Hetty and Charlie could hear the muffled sounds of Ida, Bernard, and Herman
struggling to get inside.

"I believe," Hetty said, pointing to the cast iron toy in Charlie's
hand, "you brought that to Gent one year."

"I had to buy him a gift," Charlie said.

"Buy who?"

"Officer Talbot. He was leaving town."

"His last Christmas in Sullivan."

"Yes."

"You wanted to thank him."

"Yes."

"For what, Charlie?"

Charlie inhaled deeply, turning the cast iron toy over in his
hand. A silly little police officer, the blue paint of his uniform mostly
gone. "For not turning me in when he caught me stealing."

"What'd you steal, Charlie?"

His eyes were wet when he raised his head. "This," he whispered, holding the little toy into a stream of light.

"It comes back to you, doesn't it? Just holding it?"

In Charlie's mind, the alley door popped open, and here he came, that little boy that Charlie had once been. Barely even Walter's age. The little boy who had decided that the only way to act grown-up was to be mean. Snarling and without care. A trampler, that's what he had thought it was to be a man. Big boots and a heavy fist. A tormentor, like Frank Nash or Al Capone.

Only, when Officer Talbot had pulled him out of the store—dragging him by his shirt collar—he had taken a look at him. Square in his eye. And he had seen a mask on a little boy's face. "Big tough guy," he'd muttered with a chuckle. He knew there was a chance to slip that mask free before Charlie grew so big that it was too tight to ever wrench it off again.

That was how a lie turned true, most times. Or so Officer Talbot had said.

Officer Talbot had sentenced Charlie himself. Right there on the sidewalk. Only, the sentence had to be carried out under Officer Talbot's own set of rules and on every afternoon at his direction.

"He made me come to the station. Sweep up. Clean the floor," Charlie said. "Only, it was more like clean up my own act."

"He wanted you to see the people who were brought in. What kind of shape they were in. What kind of horrible life that could have been."

"Yes."

"There was more, though."

"We were pals," Charlie said. "He shared his lunch and he told me jokes and we had a catch."

"He showed you something."

"He showed me how to get myself together."

"He showed you something else."

Charlie didn't ask how Hetty knew this. Surely somewhere along the way, Gent had told her why the little toy had meant so much.

"When I'd finished paying my dues, he gave that toy to me," Charlie said, staring, in his mind's eye, back at that little boy he'd been. "But it felt like he was telling me I'd made it. I'd become a different sort of person. Maybe even made a step toward being a man. I'd succeeded."

"What did he show you, Charlie?"

Charlie shook his head. He wasn't going to say it.

Somebody banged against the door. Not the alley door—that one remained open, letting a bit of moonlight seep in. No, it was the door to the front of the building. More muffled voices.

"What would have happened to you if Officer Talbot had just gone by the book, Charlie? What if he'd had you sent to reform school? What if he'd decided to process you through the juvenile court?"

Those muffled voices called his name. Charlie and Hetty both looked in their direction, bothered by the desperation—but not enough to leave the speakeasy, go unlock the front door.

"It would have destroyed me," Charlie said. "I really was—a tenderheart."

"What would you have done?"

"Part of me thinks I would have crumbled. The other part thinks—I would have toughened up."

"In a good way, Charlie?"

Charlie looked back at his younger self. "Most times, I think I would have been angry. Wanted to hit back. You get punched, you punch back. So—no. Not in a good way."

"Don't you think *that* was why you didn't haul in Maxwell Ross? The one who wanted Frankie to buy his liquor? The one who called her speakeasy in on Christmas Eve? You didn't want him to punch back."

"I picked wrong," Charlie said.

"Oh, Charlie. Come on, now. Tell me. What did Officer Talbot show you?"

A tear welled up in Charlie's eye as he thought of Tom. And Walter. He thought of buying the boy shoes, turning it into a little game. Payment for services.

"What, Charlie? What did he show you? When you left that toy with Gent, and you got money for a gift, what would that little boy have said about Officer Talbot? What would he have said he did for him?"

Charlie looked deep into the memory of himself. And he knew what that little boy would have said. He knew—but so much time had passed. And it didn't matter what Hetty was trying to get him to say out loud. He *had* picked wrong.

The voices of the outside world grew more insistent.

Charlie stood.

The young boy—the memory of who Charlie had been all those years ago—stared right at him. And Charlie knew—all those things that had sneaked up on him lately, those things about the town that he had not noticed before that very day, the drabness and the lack of Christmas spirit—it was not that he'd simply been too busy or too wrapped up in himself. He had not been able to look too closely at it. He had not forgotten the story of the boy who had fallen through the ice of the Pendleton pond, the one Ida had reminded him of, his drowning taking away winter skates from then on. Charlie had not been able to haul it from the tucked-away crevice of his memory.

He could not bear it, any of it.

He was even still a tenderheart. That boy he had been was not so very gone.

Yet again, music began to play. A piano, but distant that time. Not the same boisterous sounds he had heard when he'd stepped inside. It was suddenly closing time, Frankie gathering up all the glasses.

"Why did you put the speakeasy on your list?" Charlie asked Hetty. "Was it only about the music box? Or something more?"

"You know, I think this old speakeasy is a lot *like* Gent's music box. I can hear melodies here that shouldn't be playing anymore—I think you can, too. And this old bar—the way it's carved up—it's like a giant version of Gent's music boxes. Like he could have made it himself. This place, Charlie, it's different. I can't explain it, but memory is alive in here. It breathes. Tell me you can't feel that."

"I can," Charlie heard himself murmur.

"There's something really unfinished about all of this. Something that *shouldn't* be finished. If you expose me, though, you'll kill it. Do you want to kill it?"

A shadow swooped in through the alley, landing on the very bar that Hetty'd spoken of. The shadow, though, was attached to a red bird who cocked his head at Charlie and Hetty. Inexplicably—when he should have been in a tree, nesting until dawn.

"Cardinals appear when angels are near," Hetty recited.

"Officer Talbot used to say that," Charlie said.

"Did he, now?" Hetty asked, her voice nearly getting drowned out by the knocking and the shouting of the three still trying to get into the building.

"Wasn't he your guardian angel, Charlie? Who's angel are you going to be now?"

Charlie squeezed the toy. He really could still hear the piano. And, somewhere underneath it all, the echo of gunshots seven years gone.

"What are you going to do, Charlie?" Hetty asked.

220

40.

A S SOON AS HETTY finished asking her question, memories grew hazy. The past faded enough for the present to shine through.

In a great cluster of feet and hands and trying to be the first over the threshold, the door to the back portion of Frankie's old restaurant burst open. Had Charlie not seen the key shining in Herman's hand, he might have believed they'd knocked that door down rather than unlocked it. The three of them—Ida, Bernard, and Herman—all charged forward, their voices a swarm of bees.

Charlie smiled at them from where he sat, alone at the bar.

Bernard let out a kind of muffled yelp. He could not see Hetty. He couldn't see much, actually. It was dark in that back room. It smelled like weathered wooden storage boxes and time long gone by.

But fear was a funny thing—especially fear mixed with guilt. That particular cocktail could cloud the vision, far worse than the strongest moonshine. And at that moment, it was keeping Bernard from seeing Hetty's faint outline, hiding in a bleak back corner, Gent's music box in her hands.

Her eyes sparkled back there—but eyes always did, when they were in the midst of becoming a magical ingredient.

"I don't know what's going on here, Charlie," Herman said. "*These* two were outside, pawing at the front door like there was just something they had to get at. I don't know that they weren't here before."

"Oh, now, Herman, I told you what that was all about," Ida babbled, while Bernard took a step toward Charlie.

But Charlie was looking at the little cast iron toy in his hand. What would Charlie do now? Follow the rules? Tell Herman? Expose Hetty? Bring her in? For what? Breaking and entering, obviously. But what else had she done? What was the harm?

What could *he* harm, by simply making the wrong decision again?

Ida tried to catch Charlie's eye. The answer, she thought, was simple.

But it wasn't. Not to Charlie. Not with so many questions still hanging in the air.

Would Hetty continue this work of returning items? And what of the rest of it—this silliness about a music box and an inheritance? Was he really going to play along with this? With *all* of this? Was he going to drag poor Walter to Hetty's funeral? Was he going to honor Hetty's nonsensical wishes? To what end? Hadn't he dragged Walter around enough?

Right there, that night, at that moment, Charlie Barister had the fate of the entire town in his hands.

But he wasn't the only one.

Hetty knew everything was going to hinge on this Christmas.

This December, this holiday season.

If only, Hetty thought, the town would come to believe it.

In the darkness, Hetty opened Gent's music box.

223

41.

THAT OLD MUSIC BOX should not have done anything. Everyone knew *broken* meant a past tense. It meant over. It meant that
it should have had no power.

But then again, neither should old women. Or lowly house-
keepers or cooks. Or ten-year-old boys. Or cast iron toys.

And yet, all of it was mixing together. All those ingredients.
In a way that it hadn't quite before. Together, everything that had happened the past few days was turning an invisible key in the music box.

A music that could not be heard—only felt—began to pour
from Gent's music box. A melody unlike any even Hetty had experi-
enced opening the box. It sent ripples through the speakeasy and out
the alley door.

And it began to make ripples all through town.

It touched Mrs. Drummond, standing in her snow-covered
front yard and holding her mother's old mirror. It touched her as she
marveled at how close it all felt—losing her father, and her mother's

determination, and the hardening of her own tenderhearted ways. So close that it seemed that memory was itself a kind of artificial respiration for the past. So close, it seemed that the past still existed as long as memory was around to breathe for it.

It touched Walter, too, and Petey, watching Mrs. Drummond soften. It touched Rose, who lifted her hand from her switchboard long enough to bring her fingertips to the pearl she still wore on that kite string. It touched James at the drug store, so that it made him retreat to his office to double-check that his uncle's letter opener was still there, behind the lock on the top drawer. It touched Mrs. Rossi, who placed the ring from the strange woman—the same appraised by Mr. Rosenbaum—behind the loose brick in the fireplace and instructed Elizabeth to never tell her father it was there. And it touched Mr. Rosenbaum, who checked the watch on his wrist and saw that he had plenty of time left in his evening. Far more than he'd originally thought. And he smiled at the next person in line.

It touched a man out there at the Hooverville, too. The man who took one last look at the photo that had been brought to him Thanksgiving night. He cinched up his knapsack and tossed it over his shoulder. The train whistle was blowing. Time to get a move on.

And it touched Charlie.

Ida could tell just by looking at him, sitting there with that little cast iron toy in his hand.

All over town—in the speakeasy and far beyond—memories were breathing again. Here they were, long-gone grandmothers and aunts and sons. Their dreams and their struggles, they were back, in drawers and in pockets and in pocketbooks and hanging on walls. Hetty's trinkets had brought them all back to life, by simply casting a light on their memory.

But with Gent's music box playing again, something else began to breathe right alongside the memories—though no one understood it right then. It was a promise. A promise of a magical place, where the past could come to life. Right there, at the site of Frankie's old speakeasy, where Gent's broken music box was sending out its vibrations, the tuneless melody seeping into the brick.

Someday, they would have such a place.

But only if they all kept going—if only they would continue to hang on to memories they had found again this holiday. If only they would remember the magic of a stranger's kindness.

Gent and Hetty both knew how kindness could change a landscape.

The music played on.

The magic played on.

42.

MEMORIES WERE NOT BREATHING for Herman, though. He had received no such trinket—no lost family heirloom. No great story and unexpected gift like the Rossis.

"Well?" Herman asked Charlie. "You find anything out yet?"

Charlie offered a kind of gentle smile. "Yes," he said, pulling himself from the bar. "You did have an intruder."

"I knew it," Herman said, wiping his forehead.

Ida stopped breathing. Was Herman's inability to feel Gent's music going to disrupt everything?

"I saw her not long before you showed up," Charlie said.

Bernard took another step forward.

"Right over there," Charlie said, pointing toward the back of the old speakeasy.

Hetty clutched Gent's music box tighter. Was he pointing at her?

But it couldn't be, Ida thought. Why, Charlie was already

primed to go against the rules already—it was why he tried looking inside that old ice house without permission. Surely, he wasn't about to backtrack, retreat back behind that starched collar. Not now.

"Who?" Herman demanded, his arms out from his sides. "It was a her? Some tramp from the Hooverville send his woman in here to rob me?"

"Well, that depends on if the Hooverville has raccoons," Charlie said.

"A raccoon?" Herman repeated.

Ida exhaled.

Bernard's shoulders relaxed.

In the dark corner, Hetty smiled.

"Chased her out of here," Charlie said. "I was afraid there might have been more. That's why I had that alley door open. Just trying to make sure."

"Raccoons," Herman said again.

"Listen, now," Ida told Herman, "I want to talk to you about the Pendleton job."

"What Pendleton job is that?" Charlie asked.

"Bernard and I were coming out here because the Pendletons want to serve that pudding of his at their big Christmas shindig."

"They are!" Charlie said. "That's great news."

"What's so great about it?" Herman growled. "I lose a restaurant and you think one lousy party's going to make up for it?"

"You've never been to a Pendleton party, then," Ida said.

Herman shrugged and shook his head.

"You would not believe the people that show up. I don't mean numbers. I mean the—the—"

"I believe the word you're looking for is highfalutinness," Bernard chimed in.

"Yes!" Ida said, laughing. "I believe that's right."

"One good job suddenly leads to ten," Charlie said. "The people that go to Pendleton parties all throw parties themselves."

"Huh," Herman said, chewing on the inside of his cheek, thinking.

"Listen, Ida," Charlie said, "why don't you and Herman go talk this over out front? Bernard and I'll take a look at this alley door here and make sure it's all good and tight so no more critters will be able to worm their way in."

Easily led by the promise of money, Herman followed Ida out of his defunct restaurant.

In the quiet of the old speakeasy, Charlie offered an assuring smile at Bernard.

Hetty closed her music box and stepped from the darkened corner.

Bernard snatched his old friend up in his arms.

43.

AS THOUGH IN CELEBRATION, the sparkle on the stars intensified all through town, adding enough light to even make the snow in-between footprints sparkle a bit. That sparkle made Walter think of the light he'd seen in the stranger's eyes the night before.

"See, Mom?" he asked, pointing to the mirror. "She wasn't trying to steal anything. That woman the other night wanted to bring this back."

Mrs. Drummond looked down at Walter, her eyes round with surprise. He braced himself for another attack, for some scolding, some look of annoyance on her face that he was being too tender again.

"Yes," was all she murmured.

Of all things. His own mother. Told the very same thing. And the way she kept looking at that mirror assured him that somewhere, deep inside, that tender heart of hers was still beating.

When Mrs. Drummond realized there were two boys in the

yard, she said, "Did you need something, Petey?"

Petey was feeling his own version of shell-shocked, having felt the vibrations from Hetty's broken music box himself. He could only look at her, dumbfounded. "I—" He turned to Walter, trying to figure out what he wanted to say.

And as proof that somehow, some change was underfoot—that the ripples of the Bonwit kindness were etching themselves into Sullivan in a more permanent way, Petey said, "I came to see if you had a hammer, Walt. I was going—I was thinking—maybe we could put Mrs. Bonwit's mailbox back on her porch. I—accidentally—knocked it off today."

"If you have to," Mrs. Drummond said, some of her previous harsh tone returning.

"Walter," she added, "I'll hold your dinner for you."

44.

TWO DAYS LATER, HETTY Bonwit jiggled about in the front seat of the Model T. How was it her hinges had gotten so rusty that even the bumps in the road could now offer discomfort?

"I apologize, Mrs. Bonwit," Bernard said, gripping the steering wheel tighter. "It's a rough stretch of road here. Perhaps, if we could save enough, I could get Grady at the garage to install some of those *shock absorbers.*" He emphasized the words, as he did anything newfangled—offering both a hint of awe and disgust at the same time.

Hetty chuckled, tugging the blanket tighter around her mid-section. (How could it be possible to be so very *cold,* even inside the Model T, locked away from the December chill?) "I believe, Bernard," she said, "that if you and I are ever to be on a permanent first-name basis, it should be now."

"Now, ma'am?"

"Yes, after having delivered all the trinkets. After spending all the money I received from Elizabeth Rossi on groceries to leave on their stoop. After—" Her voice wound down again. After what? After completing the last of her life's work together? She grimaced again. Always before, at the end of a job, another opened up before a person. But here, at this moment, Hetty Bonwit was coming to the last few sentences. The page that would turn next would be her last.

"So sorry, ma'am," Bernard apologized again, interpreting her grimace as one of dissatisfaction or discomfort with the bumps and lurches of the Model T. Bernard tightened his jaw. "*Hetty*," he corrected himself, and offered her a smile so awkward she could do nothing but laugh. She held her stomach, as though she might break into a hundred different tiny little parts.

The laughter wound down as they grew close to the square. Defensively, she felt herself bristle. It had been ages since she had been out and about in Sullivan. So long—why, she was almost a stranger, here. Did she recognize any of those faces? Her eyes seemed cloudier than ever, but—would she even know these faces with perfect vision? How could she have retreated so far inside herself?

Perhaps, part of her thought, that meant that *they* would not recognize *her.* And perhaps that was itself a gift.

It did not feel like one, though. It felt like a wound for a wound, which was no way to live.

"What are they building?" Hetty asked, pointing to the workers bustling along the square.

"Just putting the tree up," Bernard told her.

"The tree?"

"For the lighting ceremony."

"I didn't think we would have one this year," Hetty said wistfully.

"New development," Bernard told her as he steered the Model T to a stop. "It was in the paper yesterday morning. The parade is back on, as well."

Hetty's mouth spread into a satisfied grin. "Gent's music box worked quite a few wonders, didn't it?"

"Oh, Mrs.—Hetty. It wasn't only the box. It was you." Bernard killed the engine. And he reached for the music box in Hetty's lap. But he could not look her in the eye.

That box contained instructions Bernard had helped Hetty craft for the inheritor. They both knew of the power of the music box—but it would take something special indeed to convince anyone else.

"You must also take this with you," Hetty said, handing an envelope over to Bernard.

"What is this?" he asked.

"My instructions. For the house. After I'm gone."

When Bernard began to protest she said, "I had to make sure there would be arrangements for you, yes?"

He took in a deep breath. "I had not expected—"

"Well, of *course* you didn't expect. But I need someone to be there to take care of Reginald," she said with a wink.

Bernard had only begun to smile when she said, "In return, I ask you again not to come to my funeral."

"Hetty, please—"

"It is part of the plan," Hetty insisted.

Bernard clenched his jaw, making the muscles bulge on each side of his face. He relented with nothing more than a silent, brief nod.

Yes, Bernard had always known about the strength of the Bonwits' kindness. That, as far as Bernard was concerned, was the most important engine behind what was gearing up to be a lovely Sullivan Christmas.

Hetty watched him get out of the car and walk toward the building, Gent's box tucked under his arm.

And she knew—he would march down to the basement of the Bank of Sullivan. He would find Gent's attorney—Mr. Pulcheck, Esquire, a distant carriage house guest himself. And he would rap his knuckles on the office door. And Mr. Pulcheck, who himself would always feel a debt to Mr. Bonwit, would see the music box first, before he saw Bernard. And he would sigh with relief and joy. "Finally," he would say.

Hetty knew this, even though she did not have enough energy to walk down to the basement. A few days ago, she had made it through the woods. Now, that seemed Herculean.

She tilted her head back, watching the workers on the square busily hoisting the tree upright on its trunk.

"Someday," she murmured, "there will no longer be any bad feelings associated with that old speakeasy."

It was her final wish to her hometown.

45.

THE TINSEL ARRIVED, AS no one had initially believed it would.
It arrived wrapped about wreaths made in church basements. It arrived accompanied by old Santa boots polished up to look shiny again. It arrived with fabric bows hand-died red. It arrived with crepe paper decorations in display windows on the square.

It arrived to be draped in scallops around the town tree, donated by the Pendletons themselves, cut straight from the woods beside their home.

The Sullivan High band played "Deck the Halls," their trumpets and trombones shining like festive gold bells there after sunset, in the warm yellow glow from the incandescent streetlights.

Tom squealed, up on Charlie's shoulders. Occasionally, the thrill of it all overwhelmed him and he kicked a little at Charlie's chest. The heels of those little boy shoes could pack quite a wallop, but it wasn't intended to hurt, and Charlie didn't mind. His excitement was what Charlie had always wanted. Tom's excitement had been warm in

Charlie's veins all morning.

The Christmas spirit bubbled through the square. The holiday was underway, as Charlie had once feared it would not be.

When Charlie saw him—the one person he had hoped to see here—he placed Tom on the sidewalk, put his little hand in his mother's. Tom fussed a bit—he'd never see here, not like he could on Charlie's shoulders.

Charlie simply picked up the little cast iron toy Tom had dropped—the police officer Charlie himself had loved—and placed it back in his hand. He put a finger to his lips. "It's a game," he whispered. "I'm going down low, too. You stay right here."

Hunched over, his chest nearly on his thighs, Charlie wove through the crowd.

Until he got to him. The little boy looking even younger than his ten years in clothes far too big for him. With his family. In full sing-along.

The singing stopped, though, when Charlie tapped his shoulder. "Can I talk to you a minute?" he asked.

Petey's eyes swelled with fear at being singled out by a policeman. No adult ever asked him for anything. They only ignored him or got after him.

"It's okay. I just need to ask you a favor. About Walter."

"He's with his parents," Petey said, pointing.

"No—I don't need Walter. I need to talk to you about him."

Petey's eyes shot through the crowd, over toward his friend.

"Don't let on we're talking about him," Charlie said. "I need this to be between us."

Intrigued, Petey followed him to the back of the crowd.

"I know your dad owns the funeral home," Charlie started.

Petey nodded.

"So you have to know Hetty Bonwit has died."

"*Yeah*," Petey breathed. "They're bringing her over tomorrow. I heard Dad say. What an empty funeral that one's going to be. No one's going to come. Dad's already worried about it. He takes it personally or something when hardly anyone shows. We've never had a completely empty room before. This'll be the first."

Charlie had come to suspect that deep down, the recipients of the Bonwit trinkets had all known it was Hetty. No one had said as much—perhaps they'd tried to convince themselves otherwise before letting the words out. Then again, maybe they had been a bit embarrassed at their own actions—their anger and their shaking fists at an old woman who was afraid of losing and only wanted a bit of peace. Maybe they had hoped that accepting the trinket was the last thing that needed to be said. Regardless, Charlie still didn't think that anyone was actually going to show at the funeral. Neither the still-annoyed nor the embarrassed. There was no one to make up to anymore. Funerals were always for the living.

"There is one person," Charlie said. "The only one in town who might be persuaded to come."

Petey thought for a moment. "Not Walter. That's who you really think? Come on."

"Walter's the only one kind enough." Charlie said. "I think you know what I mean."

"Tenderheart," Petey finished. "That's what his mom's always saying about him." He thought a minute. "We went out there to fix Bonwit's mailbox a few days ago. I remember, she came home while we were still working on it. That guy was with her—"

"The housekeeper? Bernard?"

Petey shrugged. "I guess so. But she acted like she was going to say something to Walter. *Get away* or something. Or maybe *let me go get my broom.* You know, so she could swing it at us and knock our blocks off. Even when we were trying to do something nice." Petey shook his head, disgusted. "I don't think even Walter would go now."

Charlie felt his stomach dip. He still didn't know what to think of Hetty's plan. In reality, it could have been the rantings of a woman at the end of her life, her mind coddled. But then again, she had already done something to Sullivan, with the return of those trinkets. Her actions had given them back their parade. This official unveiling of the Sullivan tree. The lighting ceremony was only minutes away.

Hetty had given Charlie a little trinket. But she had given something for Tom. She had made sure the town would be the same town that Charlie remembered. That was the true trinket, the heirloom.

Didn't he owe her one—even if he didn't fully understand it?

Yes, Charlie thought, he had to do this thing for Hetty. He had already gotten the deed for Frankie's old restaurant filed away properly. He trusted Bernard had placed the music box in the bank as well.

Now, all that was left was to make sure that Walter got to the funeral. That the music box—the one Hetty swore had abilities even broken—would get safely into his hands.

"I understand how she made everyone feel," Charlie said. "Trust me. But I still think Walter will go. I do, because I've seen him in action. He helped me with that strange woman in the black cloak case."

"What happened with that, anyway?" Petey wanted to know. "Did you arrest her?"

"I can't tell you that. I can't tell *anybody* that. Even Walter doesn't know the full story." Which was true. He had not told Walter that Hetty Bonwit was the woman in the black cloak. He had simply visited the Drummond house and personally thanked Walter in front of his parents. Assured them the case had been resolved.

"I got a chance to know Walter," Charlie said. Snow was beginning to trickle. It was getting in Charlie's eyelashes and dancing on Petey's cheeks. "Not as well as you do. But I do think you'll agree with me. He's the one—more than any other person in town—who would go to the funeral."

"Yeah, probably." Petey shook his head like he couldn't quite believe his friend. "Why do you even want somebody there? That old lady was mean to everybody. I bet she was even mean to you."

Petey wanted to squint at Charlie like he was sizing him up while pulling a cigarette from his pocket. But that kind of thing worked with kids, not adults. He was a little lost here—and had to simply wait for Charlie to give him an answer.

"In a weak moment," Charlie admitted, "I promised Hetty before she died that *someone* would be at her funeral. I wouldn't let her go off into the great beyond alone."

"Boy," Petey said, rolling his eyes. "That was a doozy."

Charlie smiled, enjoying this camaraderie. How long had it been since someone in town had talked to him this willingly? Not just offering information, but a little something of themselves?

"I really think Walter is our man. Besides," Charlie said, nudging Petey like they were pals themselves, "it gets you off the hook. Your old man won't insist *you* stay."

Petey's face brightened. It felt good to Charlie to lift him that way.

"Don't make a fool out of me, okay, bud?" Charlie asked.

The word zinged like an arrow, straight out of Charlie's mouth and into the softest parts of Petey. "I would never do that," he whispered. He knew how important it was.

"I can count on you, then. To do this thing for me—and for your dad?" Charlie held out his hand.

"It won't be easy," Petey warned him.

Charlie pushed his hand closer.

"All right," Petey moaned. "I'll help. You can count on me."

They shook on it.

A done deal.

The crowd around them gasped. Petey stood on his toes and craned his neck. Charlie turned.

And there it was, glowing under the December sky: Christmas, in all its tinsel-wrapped, lit-up glory.

IT WAS A TEMPT of fate. Both of them knew it as they stepped out from the speakeasy portion of the building, into the front. *Just for a peek*, that's what they'd said. A hint at what the town looked like, here, a few weeks before Christmas.

It was night of the tree lighting ceremony, after all. How could they miss that?

"What if someone notices we're here?" Hetty whispered.

"Oh, my dear," Gent said, "they're far too wrapped up in themselves to see anything else tonight."

"Must be cold," Hetty observed. "Not a single head without a hat. Mittens galore."

There was no need for either of them to have such concerns, not anymore. But there was a wistfulness in Hetty's voice. *Remember the sting of ice, the burn of a snowball in your palm?* right there in her tone.

"I remember our Christmas wedding," Gent said. "The smell of flowers in the parlor. The draft leaking through the front windows.

The piano chords and the flush of your cheeks."

There had also been a feeling of being locked up safe from the rest of the world that day—the crackle of the fireplace, the closeness of family. But that feeling of being bottled up, tucked away from the rest of the world was here, too. It had been each night since Hetty's passing. Just the two of them, their heads an inch apart as they shared a table in the back.

There were others, of course. The same regulars Gent had spoken of when Hetty had discovered him in the speakeasy. But at their table, they were walled off from everything. Love could do that when it was a fresh bloom.

"I do wish we had the music of that music box," Hetty commented.

"My dear, you play a mean piano."

"I do not," Hetty argued, "but it's all we have."

"For now," Gent corrected.

"For now," she relented.

Voices filtered in from the street—an entire town joining in on the Sullivan High band's rendition of "Silent Night."

Hetty cocked her head to the side, a glass of sherry in her hand. "It really is a lovely tree."

Gent nodded, the lights draped around the spruce casting a glow on his face.

The two stood in the window, absorbing the scene. Funny—they knew more at that moment than they ever had about Sullivan. But such was the way of departures. A person never fully understood a time in their life until it came to a close.

They knew that Walter was looking into the glow of the tree and thinking of how everything had changed in so little time—since the day he had spent with Officer Barister. How he felt he could walk anywhere, in his new shoes, and how there was no need to worry about being yelled at for crossing near the Bonwit house, not anymore. But really, he had already not been worrying. And he had been a little sad to hear the Bonwit woman had died.

They knew that when Charlie patted Petey's shoulder, for a brief moment, he heard something—not exactly the high-pitched notes of a music box, but something not unlike what had buzzed against his ears that night in the speakeasy. It was vibrating deep inside of him again. And Gent and Hetty knew that it was not his imagination. That box really was open, deep in the confines of the bank. They knew that Mr. Pulcheck, Esquire, was in the midst of locking up for the night, shaking his head as he put on his coat. And then, as was his custom each evening, he was turning that music box over in his hands, almost as a way to somehow summon an inheritor.

They both knew from the look on Petey's face that the inheritor was on his way.

It was a nice, comfortable feeling. Even though so much still hung in the balance. So much depended now on a ten-year-old boy's decisions.

Such a funny place to be—dependent on a little boy.

"I'm so glad you gave them all their trinkets back," Gent said. "I knew I had to give them a way to pay me. And I wanted to find a way to get those things back to them, but…I never could figure it out."

"I'm glad you didn't before this Christmas. It would never have worked out the same, I think," Hetty said, watching the twinkling lights settle on Gent's face.

"How long will it be before we see the work pay off?" Hetty asked. Meaning—how long until someone new would join them, or something would change at their newly acquired address, the site of the old speakeasy. How long before Walter's actions might—*fingers crossed*—begin to make some additional alterations right there in town.

"Many years, I'm afraid," Gent said. Then, as he picked up her hand to kiss it, "Trust me. It can be a lovely thing to wait, especially when you know what's coming is beautiful."

245

Present Day

"ARE YOU?" RUSS PRESSES. "An ingredient? In the magic that exists here?"

Hetty has said too much, certainly. She does not want to talk to a journalist. For decades, Hetty Bonwit has silently relished the fact that the nastiest old woman in all of Sullivan was also the one who had set the stage for Ruby's Place existing at all. Her instructions to Charlie, her funeral, the music box, the deed that sat waiting until Ruby Westbrook returned to her hometown…it all ensured that Christmas could never leave Sullivan behind. It laid the foundation for Christmas Eves here, at what is now a lovely little supper club. Where one night a year, the living could reunite with a long-lost loved one, tell them everything they hadn't had a chance to say before they passed—*I'm sorry* or *I love you*. None of it would have ever been possible without her.

Which meant, perhaps, that in her declining years, the weakest Sullivan resident had also been the strongest. That's how she likes to think of it, anyway.

"An ingredient?" Hetty repeats. She cocks her head back and gulps down the rest of her drink. When she places her hand on the bench beside her, she finds a thick coating of snow.

Is she an ingredient? It's an interesting question. What *is* she now? Why, nothing more than a memory. That's how Christmas Eve at Ruby's Place works, after all. Yes, Ruby's Place—the supper club that had come to be decades after the speakeasy had closed. At Ruby's on Christmas, memories come to life.

"Don't you know, by now, everyone in this town is an ingredient?" she tells Russ. It's a sidestep. But it's also true. Without Walter, or Elizabeth, or Charlie…without Ruby, the right person to finally, nearly twenty years after Hetty's passing, buy the old building…

These thoughts keep circling back again, like the cylinder inside a music box, playing her favorite melody.

Russ only nods at her, his jaw set askew. He knows there's more, but also recognizes that this is all the answer she will give him. He has no time to press her. Tonight, there is also his own story, playing out for him just behind the doors. There is his own hope that once inside, he will finally reach his own peace.

That hope does draw him back inside, and she is left alone again.

She closes her eyes, letting the snow dance on her face. She likes to absorb the sounds of the season: the cars and the voices and the click of heels on pavement. The hurry to be where the festivities are. The feeling that there is suddenly a need to race, to get there before the magic fades.

"Hello?" A voice interrupts her thoughts. "Hello, I said?"

"Back yet again, are you?" Hetty asks, her eyes still closed.

When Russ doesn't answer, she cracks her eyes. But she finds a different face staring at her.

"My dear, you've been keeping me waiting for quite some time."

"Oh, posh," Hetty says as Gent sits beside her. "You know I don't go inside on Christmas Eve."

"Aren't you ever going to take credit for your hand in this place?" Gent asks.

"Our hands," Hetty corrects.

"I would never take credit without you."

"I know." She nudges him with her shoulder. "It's the only drawback to keeping quiet. But if it's any consolation, our friend Walter thinks it was more about you than me."

"No consolation at all, my dear," Gent says.

It's not over, though. Gent will keep at this; he will want her to go in, take credit for her role all those years ago. Hetty merely shrugs and says, "I'm here, aren't I? Isn't that proof that someone does, in fact, remember?"

Gent chuckles quietly as he takes her hand.

"I like to think of this place—Ruby's Place—as our new carriage house. Where people who need something—relief, closure—can find it."

"It's a nice way to think of it," Gent agrees, nostalgia in his voice.

Still more revelers race down the street, always in laughing clumps.

One such clump is talking of Ruby's Place as they grow close.

"He's heard stories about it," one woman is telling her friends, wagging her thumb at the man at her side. She wears a playful grin, a disbelieving grin, the kind that says she is well aware that this story is no more than an urban legend. A silly little myth for Christmas, not unlike Santa Claus himself.

"They say it's where the past come alive," her companion says. The sheepish way about him says he believes in it, even though he knows he shouldn't.

"Where did you hear this?" he's asked.

"From someone—someone who—" he glances over at the woman at his side, his hesitance saying that he knows he'll catch flack for what he is about to say. He gathers up strength enough to finish, "Someone who said it makes you feel young, you know? The possibility of it. Like that sweet, tender part of yourself is still around."

His words reverberate through Gent and Hetty, just as powerfully as the old broken music box had reverberated through the entire town on a December night so many years ago.

When the door falls shut behind the group, Gent and Hetty raise their glasses, both freshly filled, without explanation. They clink the edges together, toasting that idea—*the sweet tender part of yourself.*

This Christmas Eve reminds Hetty of the clattering mechanical toys of her youth—the cars and the voices and the gifts and the laughter. Each swing of the entrance brings bursts of boisterous harmonies.

Hetty and Gent settle deep into the bench, beneath the red glow of the club's neon sign, knowing that yes, here, at Ruby's Place, tenderness—and the remembrance of all the tenderhearts that had come before—would always shine as brightly as tonight's Christmas moon.

Come Back to Ruby's

Want to know what happened next with Walter and the music box?
Find out in *Tinsel Town*.

*...Or would you like to start
at the very beginning of the story?*

The original four-book Ruby's Place Christmas Collection begins when Angela finds herself stumbling onto the past, and deciding that the very best Christmas present would be one more moment spent with a long-lost loved one. She soon learns that at Ruby's Place, the "spirits" are not confined to the dusty liquors behind the bar, and that the Christmas wish to see a special someone one more time is never made in vain.

Christmas at Ruby's

I Remember You

Sentimental Journey

The Gift That Is Ruby's Place

Once I'd wrapped the original series, I just could not let Sullivan go. Not when so much story was left. So I started the Ruby's Regulars series. *Ruby's Story* tells the tale of how Ruby came to open her supper club. Each subsequent book focuses on a new regular: Elizabeth in *Rare Gems* and Walter in *Tinsel Town*. In *A Troublesome Heart*, the focus is on the very first regulars, those who occupied the building even before Ruby returned to town.

Ruby's Story

Rare Gems

Tinsel Town

A Troublesome Heart

Holly Schindler

Holly Schindler is an author of books for readers of all ages. Her books have received starred reviews in PW and Booklist and have won both the silver medal in Foreword INDIES Book of the Year and the gold medal in the IPPY Awards. She is currently drinking too much coffee and singing carols far too loudly as she writes her next Ruby's Place installment.

Check out her socials, see the full list of published books, or subscribe to her newsletter at:

HollySchindler.com